WORTH THE WAIT

A SECOND CHANCE ROMANCE

WORTH IT ALL
BOOK 2

LIZ DURANO

She built an empire without him. Now he wants a second chance to deserve her.

Four years ago, Cameron Judd chose family approval over Lianne Peralta. Now she's LA's premier luxury event planner—and he's her newest client.

The $2 million Sterling Industries gala could make her career. Working with the man who broke her heart could destroy it.

Cameron claims he's changed, that he'll fight for her this time. But a lifetime in foster care taught Lianne she's temporary—that eventually, people see something wrong and send her away. When her own fears threaten their second chance, she must choose: let trauma protect her from heartbreak, or be brave enough to believe she deserves to be chosen.

This time, words won't be enough. He'll have to prove some love is worth fighting for—and she'll have to fight her own demons to accept it.

1

Lianne

THE STERLING INDUSTRIES logo gleams from glass doors as my business partner Amanda Gardner and I step out of the elevator. Three months ago, one of Los Angeles' top event planners if not the best, Morrison Events, imploded mid-planning, leaving their fiftieth anniversary gala in chaos. After three presentations, each opportunity moving us forward in the running, this is it.

Today, Luminous Events signs the contract that will change everything. That is, if Sterling Industries chooses us.

"Ready?" Amanda asks, her hand hovering over the door handle.

I smooth my emerald blouse, the silk cool against my palms despite the nervous heat flooding my body. Four years of eighteen-hour days, impossible clients, and proving myself in a world that loves to count out foster kids. Every success, every five-star review, every event that exceeded expectations—it all leads here.

To a two-million-dollar contract with a Fortune 500 company.

My reflection stares back from the glass doors—professional, composed, the armor I've perfected over years of walking into rooms where I don't quite belong. Dark hair pulled back in a sleek bun. Minimal jewelry except for the small gold hoops my foster mother gave me before she died. The emerald blouse I bought specifically for this meeting because green is my power color, the shade that makes my brown skin glow and my dark eyes look fierce rather than frightened.

I push open the conference room door with my brightest smile, the one that's gotten me through countless pitch meetings. "Good morning, I'm Lianne Peralta from Luminous Events, and this is—"

The man at the head of the table turns around.

Everything stops.

My portfolio hits the floor, papers scattering across polished marble with a sound that echoes through the suddenly airless room. The noise seems to come from very far away, muffled by the roaring in my ears.

"Lianne."

Cameron Phillip Arthur Judd. Pacific Palisades royalty. The man who chose his family's approval over me.

The man who taught me that love isn't enough when you're not from the right world.

Four years. One thousand, four hundred and sixty-one days since I last saw his face. Since I heard him say my name in that particular tone—soft, almost reverent, like I was something precious he was trying to memorize.

He looks the same and completely different. Dark hair

still falls across his forehead in that way that used to make my fingers itch to push it back. Hazel eyes still change color with his mood—more green when he's happy, more gold when he's serious. The broad shoulders I used to trace in the darkness of his bedroom, memorizing the planes of muscle beneath expensive cotton sheets.

But there are lines around his eyes now, a sharpness to his jaw that wasn't there four years ago. He's lost weight, or maybe it's just that he carries himself differently—tighter, more controlled, like someone who's learned to guard himself against vulnerability.

My body betrays me. Heat floods my cheeks, my pulse hammering so hard I'm certain everyone can see it thrumming in my throat. My hands shake as I crouch to gather scattered papers, grateful for the excuse to break eye contact, to hide my face while I struggle to breathe.

This can't be happening. Not here. Not now. Not when I'm finally close to everything I've worked for.

"I..." The word dies in my throat, strangled by the pressure building in my chest.

As Jennifer Cooper and Sidney Chambers—Sterling's marketing director and communications manager—stare between us, I can almost see the speculation forming in their eyes, the questions they're too polite to ask but will definitely gossip about later.

Amanda moves to take over, but I force myself to gather the scattered papers before this becomes more of a spectacle. My fingers fumble with the presentation materials, unable to grip them properly through the trembling. A photo of the charity gala we organized last spring slides across the marble, stopping near Cameron's polished Oxford shoes.

"Let me help you." He bends to retrieve it, our fingers brushing as he hands it back.

The contact sends electricity racing up my arm, my body remembering what my mind has tried desperately to forget. The way his touch used to make me feel seen, wanted, chosen. Before I learned that chosen was temporary, conditional on circumstances I could never control.

"I didn't realize you'd be personally involved in this project, Mr. Judd." My hands shake despite my best efforts, the papers crinkling between my white-knuckled grip.

Mr. Judd. As if we're strangers. As if he didn't once know every dream in my heart, every insecurity from my childhood in the system, every fear that woke me at 3 AM when I couldn't sleep.

As if he didn't whisper promises in the dark about futures that turned out to be lies.

"It's good to see you again, Lianne." His voice is carefully neutral, each word measured and controlled in a way that suggests he's working just as hard to maintain composure.

But I catch the slight hitch in his breath when he says my name. The way his knuckles whiten as his hands grip the back of his chair. Small tells I learned to read during the year we were together, back when reading Cameron's moods felt as natural as breathing.

I don't care if it's good for him. I don't care what he's feeling.

I straighten, clutching my portfolio like armor, the leather binding pressing into my chest hard enough to leave marks. Four years since I've seen his face, heard his voice, felt the devastating pull that made me believe in fairy tales despite everything my childhood taught me about the temporary nature of love.

"Welcome, Lianne. Amanda." Jennifer extends her hand, mercifully moving past the awkward moment with professional grace. "This is our final decision meeting. Cameron is Sterling Industries' primary investor and board chair—he takes personal interest in all major initiatives."

Primary investor. Board chair. Of course he is.

The boy who used to meet me in secret, who kept our relationship carefully compartmentalized from his family obligations, has grown into a man who sits at the head of Fortune 500 boardrooms. Who makes decisions that affect thousands of lives. Who probably hasn't thought about me in years except as an unfortunate chapter in his youth, a phase he outgrew on his way to becoming someone important.

"Well, I'm confident Luminous Events can exceed your expectations."

Cameron's gaze stays on my face, intense enough that I feel it like a physical touch. "I'm sure you can. Your company has built an impressive reputation."

The words should feel like validation. Instead, they feel like condescension. Like he's surprised that the foster kid he dated in secret managed to build something real, something that matters.

I ignore the way his words settle over me, the way they make something in my chest tighten with old hurt and new anger. He doesn't get to be proud of what I've accomplished without him. He doesn't get to act like my success reflects well on his judgment when he was the one who decided I wasn't worth fighting for.

"Thank you," I say coolly, taking the seat across from him. Distance. Professional boundaries. No eye contact that lasts longer than necessary. No acknowledgment of the history that pulses between us like a living thing, demanding attention we can't afford to give it.

Amanda settles beside me, her presence a reminder that I'm not alone, not the vulnerable girl who let his family make her feel small. I'm a successful businesswoman with a partner who believes in me, a company we started with a few hundred dollars and a dream, a reputation we've built through talent and determination rather than connections or privilege.

"Shall we begin?" I open my portfolio with hands that have finally stopped shaking, though my pulse still races beneath carefully applied foundation. "Our proposal addresses all your previous concerns."

For the next hour, I do what I do best.

I paint a picture of an unforgettable evening that honors Sterling Industries' fifty-year legacy while showcasing their innovation. The "Legacy and Innovation" theme balances respect for their history with excitement about their future—a delicate equilibrium that requires understanding both where they've been and where they're going.

I walk them through venue options, each one carefully selected based on extensive research into Sterling's brand identity. The Beverly Hills Hotel's Crystal Ballroom, with its iconic pink facade and Old Hollywood glamour. An exclusive Santa Barbara estate with ocean views that suggest both stability and endless possibility. Each option comes with detailed floor plans, capacity analyses, parking logistics, and contingency plans for everything from unexpected weather to last-minute guest additions.

The catering menus blend classic elegance with contemporary flair—tasting stations that honor their corporate history while showcasing innovation. Passed hors d'oeuvres that reference their founding in the manufacturing sector while highlighting their evolution into tech and renewable energy. Wine pairings that tell a story of growth and adaptation.

Entertainment concepts that will have guests talking for months—not just generic corporate band playing covers, but a carefully curated experience that reflects Sterling's journey. String quartet during cocktail hour transitioning to jazz ensemble, culminating in a surprise performance by an artist whose career they've supported through their arts foundation.

Under normal circumstances, I'd be flying on creative energy, thrilled by the possibilities, feeding off the clients' excitement as they start to envision their event coming to life.

But nothing about this is normal, because Cameron sits three feet away, and every time I glance up from my materials, I find him watching me with an intensity that makes my skin prickle with awareness.

He doesn't contribute much, mostly listening while Jennifer and Sidney ask questions about timeline, logistics, vendor relationships. But when he does speak, his questions are thoughtful, insightful—the kind that come from genuine engagement rather than performative interest.

"The networking component is crucial," he says during layout discussion, leaning forward with his forearms on the table in a posture I remember from countless business dinners we shared when we were together. "Sterling serves clients who rarely get face time with our executive team. This should feel exclusive but approachable—create genuine connection opportunities rather than forced networking pressure."

It's a good point, the kind that comes from understanding corporate dynamics and human psychology in equal measure. The kind of observation that reminds me why I fell for him in the first place—not just because he was beautiful, but because he was smart in ways that challenged me to be sharper, more strategic.

"Absolutely," I agree, making notes in my portfolio while refusing to let our eyes meet for too long. "We can create intimate conversation areas within the larger space. Comfortable seating clusters that encourage organic interaction. Subtle cues that guide people toward connection without the awkwardness of traditional networking events. Natural opportunities for conversation that feel spontaneous rather than orchestrated."

"Lianne has an incredible gift for reading social dynamics," Sidney tells Cameron. "The charity gala she organized last spring raised over three million dollars because she understood exactly how to make people comfortable while encouraging generosity. She created an atmosphere where saying yes felt natural rather than pressured."

Warmth spreads through my chest at the compliment, momentarily overriding the discomfort of Cameron's presence.

"Three million?" Cameron's eyebrows rise, genuine surprise crossing his features. "That's remarkable."

"It was a team effort," I say quietly. "For a good cause. The children's hospitals needed equipment upgrades desperately. Sometimes people just need the right environment to show their generosity. The right combination of emotional appeal and social proof, comfort and inspiration."

Something shifts in Cameron's expression—a softening around his eyes that I refuse to analyze. "I'd like to review the portfolio from that event," he says, his voice dropping slightly. "For reference purposes."

Sharing my work with Cameron feels dangerously personal, but I nod because refusing would be unprofessional. "I'll include it in the comprehensive package we send over."

Twenty minutes later, we're wrapping up. As Jennifer and Sidney gather their materials, I count the seconds until I can escape this glass-walled nightmare, until I can breathe air that doesn't carry the scent of Cameron's cologne—something woody and expensive that I've never been able to forget, that still makes my stomach flip when I catch it randomly on other men.

"Thank you for the comprehensive presentation," Cameron says as I pack up. Then he pauses. "Actually, I don't need time to review anything further. Luminous Events is exactly what Sterling Industries needs."

I freeze, portfolio half-closed as Jennifer and Sidney exchange surprised glances, their professional composure briefly cracking to reveal genuine confusion.

"Mr. Judd," Jennifer says carefully, diplomatically, "we hadn't discussed making a final decision today. The standard process—"

"The decision is mine," Cameron says firmly, his tone

brooking no argument, eyes still fixed on me with an intensity that makes my skin feel too tight. "Miss Peralta's team has presented three exceptional proposals over the past month. Their vision aligns perfectly with our brand, their execution capabilities are proven beyond question, and after Morrison Events' spectacular failure, we need planners who can deliver under pressure. Luminous Events has demonstrated exactly that capability."

My heart pounds so hard I'm certain everyone can hear it. We got it. We actually got the contract that will change everything for my company, that will establish us among LA's elite event planners, that will mean financial security and industry credibility and everything I've worked toward since the day I aged out of foster care with nothing but determination and a partial scholarship.

This is everything I wanted.

So why does it feel like a trap?

"Of course," Sidney adds quickly. "We'll have contracts prepared immediately. Our legal team can have everything ready by tomorrow."

"Excellent," Cameron replies, finally releasing me from the weight of his gaze. "Miss Peralta, expect a call from our legal team first thing tomorrow morning."

"Thank you," I manage, my voice steadier than my hands. "Luminous Events won't disappoint you."

"I'm sure you won't."

The words hang between us, loaded with four years of history. With memories of promises broken and potential destroyed. With the ghost of who we were before his family's expectations proved stronger than whatever we had together.

Jennifer clears her throat. "We should let you get back to your day, Miss Peralta. Congratulations. This is going to be a wonderful partnership."

Partnership. The word feels loaded with irony.

I gather my materials, hyperaware of Cameron watching every movement. When I finally look up, his expression is carefully neutral—the board chair making a sound business decision, nothing more. No acknowledgment of our history, no hint that the woman standing before him was once the person he claimed to love more than anything.

Maybe that's easier. Maybe pretending we're strangers is the only way either of us gets through this.

Amanda and I head for the elevator in silence that feels suffocating.

As the doors slide close, the full implications hit me. We got the contract—the two-million-dollar opportunity that will establish us among LA's premier luxury planners. That will mean hiring more staff, taking on bigger projects, building the kind of company that validates every risk I took, every doubt I pushed through, every moment I wondered if leaving foster care with no safety net was the stupidest decision possible.

"Holy shit, we got it," Amanda whispers, professional composure finally cracking. "We actually got Sterling Industries."

I stare at my reflection in polished elevator doors. Professional. Composed. Successful. Everything I've worked to become since Cameron taught me that love isn't enough when you're not from the right world, when your background doesn't match their expectations, when you're someone they hide rather than someone they claim.

"That was unexpected," Amanda continues. "Usually corporate decisions take weeks. But did you guys date or something? Because the tension in that room was—"

"Ancient history," I cut her off. "Nothing that will interfere with delivering an exceptional event."

"Good. Because we just landed the biggest contract in company history. Whatever happened between you two, we can't let it affect this opportunity. This changes everything for us—the referrals alone will be worth more than the contract fee."

She's right. Luminous Events earned this through years of dedication and determination, through building a reputation one successful event at a time. I can't let my personal history derail my professional future.

I can't let Cameron Judd take anything else from me beyond what he already took four years ago.

2

___

Cameron

I can't focus.

The acquisition report from our Hong Kong office sits open on my laptop, quarterly projections and market analysis blurring together into meaningless numbers.

I've read the same paragraph four times, absorbing nothing. All I can see is Lianne's face when she walked into that conference room—the shock blanking her features before professional composure clicked into place, the way her hands shook when she picked up her scattered portfolio, papers fluttering to marble floors like wounded birds.

The cold formality in her voice when she called me *Mr. Judd.*

As if four years could erase everything we were to each other. As if the year we spent together was nothing more than a footnote in our respective histories, easily dismissed and quickly forgotten.

I deserve that. Every bit of her coldness, her distance, her refusal to look at me longer than professionally necessary. I earned all of it four years ago when I chose my family's approval over the woman who made me want to be better than I was. When I let my mother's disapproval and my father's disappointment weigh more heavily than Lianne's tears, than the future we could have built together if I'd been brave enough to fight for it.

My phone buzzes against the dark wood of my desk, the vibration loud in the silence of my office. Sharon Finnegan, my executive assistant.

SHARON:

Contracts finalized with Luminous Events. Jennifer says they're ready to begin immediately given the timeline. Need to schedule first coordination meeting ASAP.

Three months of working with Lianne. Three months of daily meetings, venue walkthroughs, vendor selections, design reviews. Three months of her treating me like a client and nothing more, maintaining the professional boundaries I shattered when I walked away from us.

Three months to prove I'm not the man who let her go.

The Santa Monica skyline glitters beyond my windows, evening descending over the city I've called home since becoming primary investor three years ago. The view used to thrill me—evidence of how far I'd come from the privileged but purposeless life my parents envisioned. Now it just feels empty, all this success hollow without anyone to share it with.

I pull up Luminous Events' website, studying the portfolio I've already memorized during sleepless nights over the past month. The children's hospital gala that raised three million dollars—elegant without being ostentatious, creating an atmosphere where generosity felt natural rather than obligatory. A tech mogul's wedding featured in *Los Angeles Magazine*, balancing intimacy with scale in ways that seemed impossible. A nonprofit fundraiser that brought in record donations through strategic emotional appeals and flawless execution.

She did it. Everything she said she'd do, everything we talked about during late-night planning sessions when we were together, she built without me.

The thought makes me proud and makes me ache in equal measure.

A knock interrupts my spiral. Sharon enters with her tablet and the expression that means I'm not going to like what she has to say—lips pressed thin, eyebrows slightly raised, the look of someone delivering news they've already predicted the recipient's reaction to.

"Jennifer mentioned you made the decision on Luminous Events rather quickly," she says carefully, settling into the chair across from my desk with practiced efficiency. "She was surprised. Usually you take at least a week to review vendor proposals, run background checks, compare multiple options."

"The presentation was exceptional," I reply, keeping my voice neutral. "No reason to delay when the choice is obvious."

Sharon's look says she doesn't buy it, her sharp eyes seeing through the careful explanation to the truth underneath. But she's too professional to push—she's been my assistant for three years, long enough to know when to probe and when to let things lie.

"The coordination schedule." She sets her tablet in front

of me, the screen displaying a color-coded calendar that looks frighteningly full. "Luminous Events is requesting daily check-ins given the compressed timeline. First meeting tomorrow at ten. Venue walkthrough on Thursday. Vendor selection sessions next week. Final design review the week after that."

Daily meetings. My chest tightens with something between anticipation and dread, excitement and terror warring for dominance.

"I'll handle all coordination directly," I say, hearing how the words sound even as I speak them—too involved, too personal for standard client-vendor relationships.

Sharon's eyebrows rise. "All of it? Cameron, that's a lot of hands-on involvement for a board chair. You have the Hong Kong expansion meetings next week, the renewable energy summit in Copenhagen, the board presentation for the Nevada solar project. Jennifer is perfectly capable of handling event logistics—it's literally her job description."

"I want direct oversight." My tone brooks no argument, sharper than Sharon deserves. "This event represents Sterling's brand at the highest level. I need to ensure every decision aligns with our objectives, maintains our reputation."

"Of course." Sharon makes notes on her tablet. "I'll let Miss Peralta's office know you'll be the primary contact point."

When she leaves, I sit back and stare at my phone, at the blank text message screen that's been haunting me for hours.

One day to figure out how to prove to Lianne that I've changed. One day before I see her again and try to earn back even a fraction of what I destroyed.

The problem is, words won't work.

I could apologize a thousand times, explain how young I was, how much pressure my family put on me, how I've regretted that choice every single day for four years. How there hasn't been a morning I didn't wake up thinking about her, wondering if she was happy, if she'd found someone who deserved her in ways I proved I didn't.

But Lianne won't believe any of it. Why should she? Talk is easy. Excuses are meaningless. Four years ago, I made promises and broke them, claimed to love her while ultimately choosing the easier path of family approval and social acceptance.

She needs to see proof—concrete evidence that I'm not the same man who let his mother's disapproval end the best thing in his life.

My phone rings, shattering the quiet contemplation. Mother's name flashes on the screen—her timing impeccable as always, as if she sensed me thinking about the past.

"Mother."

"Cameron, darling. Your father mentioned you had to leave golf early for a work emergency." Her tone suggests she doesn't quite believe the work emergency excuse, the skepticism evident in her carefully modulated voice. "I wanted to remind you about dinner tonight. The Vitales are in town—Charles and Patricia brought Isabella. She just moved back from Milan after finishing her fashion degree. Such an accomplished young woman."

Isabella Vitale. Beautiful, accomplished, from exactly the right family. The kind of strategic match my mother has been orchestrating for the past year, pushing eligible daughters of business associates in my direction with the subtlety of a bulldozer.

The old Cameron would make excuses. Would attend the dinner out of obligation while privately resenting the manipulation, smiling through forced conversation while mentally planning his exit strategy.

That Cameron let other people's expectations dictate his choices. Let family pressure override personal desires because confrontation felt impossible, because disappointing his parents seemed worse than disappointing himself.

That Cameron lost Lianne.

"I'm not interested in Isabella, Mother." The words come out firm, clear, leaving no room for interpretation.

Silence on the other end, heavy with surprise and calculation. Then: "I'm sorry, what?"

"I'm not interested in Isabella Vitale. I'm not interested in anyone you're setting me up with." I keep my voice calm but firm, the tone I use in boardroom negotiations when making final offers. "If I want to date someone, I'll find her myself. My personal life is not a business merger requiring your oversight."

"Cameron, the Vitales are important connections for Sterling Industries' European expansion. Isabella is lovely, educated, and she understands what's expected of someone in your position. She comes from our world, darling. She knows how these relationships work, what they require—"

"She understands the social expectations that come with inherited wealth," I interrupt, my patience eroding. "I know. You've explained that before. It's the same speech you gave me four years ago about finding someone 'suitable.' About how certain backgrounds and certain families made better matches than—"

I cut myself off before saying Lianne's name, before giving my mother the satisfaction of knowing this conversation is about her.

But we both know.

Another pause, longer this time. When Mother speaks again, her voice has steel underneath the sweetness, the tone she uses when expectations aren't being met. "Four years ago, you were dating that event planner. The girl from the foster system who had no understanding of our world, no family connections, no concept of what it means to be part of families like ours. Surely you're not still dwelling on that unfortunate situation. You were so young, Cameron. Young people make questionable choices they later outgrow—"

Unfortunate situation. As if Lianne was a social misstep instead of the woman I loved. As if breaking up with her was wisdom rather than cowardice, bullet dodged instead of the biggest mistake of my life.

"Her name is Lianne Peralta," I say quietly, my voice hard with suppressed anger. "And I'm not dwelling on anything. I'm simply telling you that I make my own decisions about who I date. Not you. Not Dad. Me."

"This is about her, isn't it?" Mother's voice sharpens with realization. "Cameron, that was years ago. You've built an impressive career, you're in a position of real influence now. You could have your pick of appropriate women who would complement your success, who understand what's required—"

"I made that mistake once," I cut her off, my patience finally exhausted. "Chose what you wanted over what I needed. I'm not doing it again."

"Cameron Arthur Judd, you listen to me—"

I hang up.

For four years, I've let my mother orchestrate my social life, arrange strategic dinners, push "appropriate" women in my direction with the persistence of someone who believes she knows what's best. Sure, I'd had fun playing along, never really finding anyone worth being serious with.

But that ends now.

The phone rings again immediately. I decline the call and silence it, the screen going dark like a closed door.

Then I open my email and start typing, my fingers moving with certainty I haven't felt in years.

To: Jennifer Martinez

    Subject: *Sterling Anniversary Gala - Family Involvement*

    Jennifer,

    Please note that my mother will NOT be involved in vendor coordination or planning decisions for the anniversary gala. All coordination will go through me directly.

    If she reaches out to you or the Luminous Events team, please redirect her to me. This event represents Sterling Industries' corporate brand, not personal aesthetic preferences.

    Thanks,

    Cameron

I hit send before I can second-guess myself, before the old patterns of accommodation and conflict avoidance can reassert themselves.

Next email:

To: Development Team

    Subject: *Charity Partnership Opportunity*

Team,

I'd like to explore a partnership with LA County's foster youth programs. Specifically, I'm interested in funding scholarships or mentorship opportunities for kids aging out of the system who want to pursue careers in business or hospitality.

Please research existing programs and set up meetings with relevant organizations. I want something substantial in place by end of Q2.

Cameron

Lianne always talked about how lucky I was to have resources and connections, how people with privilege had a responsibility to use it for good rather than just accumulating more wealth and status. She wanted to help foster kids like herself—give them opportunities she had to fight for alone, create pathways that shouldn't require the kind of determination and luck that got her where she is.

I can't undo the past four years. Can't give her back the time we lost, the relationship I destroyed, the trust I shattered. But I can honor what she taught me about using success for something that matters beyond profit margins and market share.

My phone buzzes with a text. Not Mother this time—Sharon.

SHARON:

Miss Peralta confirmed for tomorrow 10am.
Conference Room B. Do you need anything
prepared?

I stare at the message, my heart rate picking up at the thought of seeing her again so soon.

Tomorrow. Less than twenty-four hours before I see her again, before I start proving—through actions, not words—that I'm worth a second chance.

ME:

> Just the venue comparison files. I'll handle the rest.

I sit back in my chair and look at the legal pad covered in notes. The list of ways I failed her. The plan for becoming the man I should have been four years ago—the man who would have fought for her instead of letting family pressure win.

Even if she never gives me a second chance, I owe her this. I owe her the man who would have stood up to his family, who would have made her feel chosen rather than hidden, who would have used his privilege to support her dreams rather than letting it become another barrier between them.

I pull up her photo on the Luminous Events website one more time. Professional headshot, confident smile, dark eyes that look directly at the camera with none of the uncertainty I remember from when we first met. The woman who built an empire without me, who proved every doubt wrong, who became exactly who she said she'd be.

Tomorrow, I start proving I've changed.

Whether she believes it or not.

3

———

Lianne

"You look better," Amanda says, handing me coffee in the oversized mug I bought after landing our first six-figure contract. "More like yourself."

I don't feel better. Last night I lay awake replaying that conference room meeting, Cameron's voice saying my name with that particular softness I thought I'd forgotten, the way my portfolio hit the floor and shattered whatever professional composure I'd carefully constructed. But Amanda doesn't need to know that my sheets are still tangled from hours of restless tossing, that I've been surviving on three hours of sleep and determination.

"Jennifer Martinez called," she continues, settling into the chair across from my desk with her own coffee. "They're moving forward. Contracts by end of day, which is lightning-fast for a company that size. Usually legal review alone takes a week."

I nod, already mentally organizing the timeline. Three months to execute what Morrison Events had eight months to plan. The industry will be watching to see if we can pull this off—watching to see if Luminous Events is the real deal or just another boutique firm that crumbles under pressure.

"There's one thing," Amanda adds, her tone shifting to something more careful. "Jennifer said their board chair wants hands-on involvement. Daily briefings, approval authority for major decisions. She made it sound like he's particular about brand image, but—"

My coffee cup freezes halfway to my lips. "Daily briefings?"

"Weekly check-ins during planning phases, daily coordination in the final week." Amanda tilts her head, studying my face with the perception that makes her an excellent business partner. "Is that going to be a problem?"

Before I can answer—before I can figure out what answer wouldn't reveal too much—our receptionist's voice crackles through the intercom.

"Lianne? You have a visitor. Mr. Cameron Judd from Sterling Industries."

Coffee sloshes over the rim of my cup, hot liquid scalding my hand. I barely notice, too focused on the words that shouldn't be possible.

Cameron. Here. At my office.

Through the glass walls that make our workspace feel open and collaborative but also offer zero privacy, I can see him in reception. Perfectly at ease in a charcoal suit that probably costs more than my monthly rent, looking like he belongs anywhere he chooses to be, his presence commanding attention without effort.

What the hell is he doing here?

"Send him in," I manage, grabbing tissues for the spill with hands that refuse to steady.

Amanda raises an eyebrow but gathers her things diplomatically, her expression saying we'll definitely be discussing this later. "I'll be in my office if you need anything."

Cameron appears in my doorway before I'm ready, and I hate that my body still responds to his presence after four years. My pulse kicks up, my skin feels too warm, my breath catches in a way that has nothing to do with professional respect and everything to do with cellular memory that apparently never got the memo about moving on.

"Mr. Judd." I stand, extending my hand with practiced professionalism. "This is unexpected. I wasn't aware we had a meeting scheduled."

His handshake is firm and brief, his skin warm against mine in a way that sends electricity up my arm. Pure business contact, nothing personal, but my body doesn't seem to understand the distinction.

"We didn't. I thought it would be more efficient to discuss planning parameters in person rather than through email chains." He settles into the chair across from my desk, his movements controlled and deliberate. "Save time on the compressed timeline."

Planning parameters. Right. Because that's definitely why a billionaire board chair personally visits event planning offices instead of delegating to his staff.

"Of course. Have a seat." I gesture to the chairs across from my desk, reclaiming my territory. My control. This is my space, my company, my rules. "What parameters did you want to discuss?"

He settles in, his gaze moving around my office with interest that feels both casual and calculated—the awards on my walls, portfolio books displaying our best work, framed photos of successful events like a children's hospital gala, a tech wedding, and a nonprofit fundraiser that put us on the map.

"You've built something impressive here," he says as I force myself not to deflect, not to minimize with "I got lucky" or "I had help"—the automatic responses of someone who spent childhood learning that claiming success was arrogant when you come from nothing. But old habits die hard.

"We've worked hard."

"*You've* worked hard," he corrects, and something in my chest tightens at his refusal to let me hide behind "we."

I clear my throat. "But back to why you're here. What parameters did you want to discuss?"

As I start writing notes, Cameron leans forward, his forearms resting on his knee. "Given the significance of Sterling Industries' 50th anniversary, I'll be taking a hands-on approach to ensure the event reflects our values accurately. Daily check-ins to ensure alignment with our goals. Personal approval for all vendor selections, venue modifications, and design elements. Direct communication to streamline decision-making and maintain quality control."

I stop writing and look up, my professional patience wearing thin. "Daily check-ins? Mr. Judd, I appreciate your concern for quality, but that level of involvement is unusual for someone in your position. Don't you have actual work to do—running a company, making billion-dollar decisions— or do you have no confidence in Luminous Events' ability to deliver? Because if it's the latter, maybe you should find someone else."

He doesn't flinch, just watches me with that unreadable expression that used to drive me crazy when we were together.

"You're right," he says finally. "Daily would be excessive, and it's not about confidence in your capabilities. Your portfolio speaks for itself—the children's hospital gala alone demonstrates exceptional strategic thinking and execution under pressure."

He pauses, his expression softening slightly. "What I should have said is that I want to be involved in key decision points. Major vendor selections, venue walkthroughs, design presentations. The strategic elements that directly impact brand perception."

I set down my pen, studying him carefully. This feels like more than standard client involvement, but I can't figure out his angle. "How often are we talking?"

"Two, maybe three times per week during critical phases. Less once major decisions are locked in and we're in pure execution mode." His tone is more collaborative now, less autocratic. "I'm not interested in approving every napkin fold or centerpiece variation, Miss Peralta. I'm interested in ensuring strategic elements align with Sterling Industries' brand values and market positioning."

The explanation makes sense professionally. High-stakes corporate events do sometimes require executive involvement beyond standard delegation. But something about Cameron's intensity suggests this is personal in ways that have nothing to do with brand management.

"I understand the importance," I say carefully, choosing

my words with precision. "But I need to be clear—I don't work well with clients who micromanage the creative process. I need space to do what I do best, which is transform strategic objectives into memorable experiences. If you're going to second-guess every decision or require approval for details that should be delegated, this won't work."

Especially not when half the industry is watching to see if I can succeed where Morrison Events failed, waiting for any sign of weakness to confirm their suspicions that Luminous Events got lucky rather than earned our reputation.

"I'm not interested in micromanaging your creativity," Cameron says, his voice taking on an almost pleading quality. "I'm interested in ensuring that creativity serves our objectives effectively. I trust your artistic vision, Lianne. I just want to understand how it translates to outcomes."

Lianne. My first name slipping out despite his earlier use of "Miss Peralta." The informality should feel appropriate given our history. Instead, it feels like a wall crumbling, like professional distance dissolving into something more complicated.

Which is exactly the problem.

"Two to three times per week is manageable," I concede, making notes in my iPad while avoiding his gaze. "What does that communication look like? Meetings here or at Sterling Industries? Video calls or in-person? Morning or afternoon preference?"

"A combination makes sense. Venue walkthroughs will be off-site by necessity. Vendor presentations wherever works best—your office or ours, whichever is more convenient for scheduling. Design reviews probably work better in person where we can see materials and discuss details."

I keep my expression neutral, but my mind is calculating. This level of involvement isn't unheard of for events this size and budget. Fortune 500 CEOs sometimes take personal interest in major celebrations. Board chairs occasionally get involved when the stakes are high enough.

But most executives delegate to their teams and show up for final approvals, trusting the professionals they hired to handle details. They don't request multiple weekly meetings, personal involvement in vendor selection, direct communication that bypasses normal corporate hierarchies.

Unless there's another reason he wants to be so involved.

"That's still quite a time commitment for a board chair with global responsibilities," I observe, watching his face for tells. "Are you sure your schedule can accommodate it? Because if we establish these expectations and you can't follow through, it will compromise the timeline."

"I've adjusted my priorities," he says simply, his jaw setting with determination I recognize from business negotiations we attended together years ago. "This anniversary is important to Sterling's market positioning. It deserves my direct attention."

There's something in how he says it but I'm not going to analyze it. I'm not going to let myself wonder about motivations beyond professional obligation.

"Alright," I say, my voice carefully neutral. "Two to three meetings per week for major decisions. Amanda will coordinate with your assistant to find times that work for both calendars."

"Excellent." Cameron stands, straightening his jacket

with movements that draw my attention to his broad shoulders, the lean strength I remember from nights I shouldn't be thinking about. "I'm looking forward to working with you, Miss Peralta."

He extends his hand again. This time his fingers linger just a fraction longer than necessary, his thumb brushing across my knuckles in a caress so subtle I might have imagined it.

Not enough to be inappropriate. Just enough to remind me we have history that can't be erased by professional titles and careful formality.

I pull my hand back and move toward the door, desperate to end this interaction before my composure cracks completely. "Likewise, Mr. Judd. I'll have Amanda send over the initial timeline and vendor list by end of day."

As we walk through the main office, I'm aware of my team watching. Terry glancing up from her fabric swatches. Sandra pausing mid-phone call to stare. The interns whispering behind their computer screens.

It's not everyday we have clients show up unannounced. Not billionaire CEOs like Cameron Judd, that's for sure.

"Is there anything specific you'd like to review first?" I ask at reception. "Menu concepts? Entertainment options? Floral arrangements?"

"Venue options," he replies, the way he gazes at me making my skin prickle. "I want to understand your selection criteria and what alternatives might be available if the primary choices don't work out."

"Given the rushed timeline, I've identified additional options that could accommodate us on short notice with the scale and sophistication you require." I pull up my notes on my phone, grateful for the excuse to look at a screen instead of his face. "The Esperanza Resort in Montecito has excellent facilities and availability. I could arrange a walkthrough as early as tomorrow if you're available."

"Tomorrow works," Cameron says immediately, without checking his calendar or considering other obligations. "What time?"

The quick agreement catches me off guard. Most executives this busy require advance notice, schedule coordination, calendar shuffling. Cameron just... agrees, like visiting venues with his event planner is his top priority.

"I'll coordinate with their events team and confirm through your assistant," I say carefully.

Cameron nods, then pauses near the door, his expression shifting to something more serious. "One more thing. I want to be clear that my involvement is purely professional. I have no interest in re-litigating the past or creating awkward dynamics that would compromise the project. We're both adults, both successful professionals, and we both want this event to succeed. That's all that matters."

The statement should be reassuring—establishing boundaries, clarifying expectations, reducing potential awkwardness.

Instead, it feels like he's trying to convince himself as much as me.

"I'm glad we understand each other, Mr. Judd," I reply coolly, opening the door for him in a gesture that's polite but clearly dismissive. "The past is irrelevant to this professional arrangement. What matters is delivering an exceptional event that meets Sterling Industries' strategic objectives."

"Exactly." He smiles—polite, meaningless, the expression reserved for business acquaintances and networking events.

"I'll look forward to hearing from your office about the venue walkthrough," he says.

The door closes behind him with a soft click. I watch through the windows as he walks to a sleek black Aston Martin parked outside.

"So," Amanda appears at my elbow before Cameron's taillights are out of view. "Two to three meetings per week with the billionaire board chair who happens to be your ex-boyfriend. That's... thorough."

"It's professional," I say, defensive even as I know how it looks. "This is a two-million-dollar contract with industry-wide visibility. Of course the board chair wants to be involved."

"Right. High-touch service." Amanda's tone says she's not convinced, her expression skeptical. "Because billionaires definitely spend their valuable time visiting event planning offices to discuss parameters instead of delegating to their staff. That's completely normal and not at all about you specifically."

"Amanda—"

"I'm not judging. I'm just saying that man didn't come here to discuss napkin colors. He came here to see you." She crosses her arms. "The question is whether you're okay with that, and whether it's going to complicate things."

I want to argue, to insist she's reading too much into standard client communication. But Amanda's not wrong. Cameron's level of involvement goes beyond professional thoroughness into something more personal, and pretending otherwise won't protect me from whatever's coming.

"I'll start coordinating schedules," Amanda says when I don't respond. "Specific times or flexible availability?"

"Twice weekly for now. Wednesdays and Fridays if possible—gives us time to implement feedback between meetings." I head toward my office, needing space to process. "And Amanda? This doesn't change how we operate. Cameron Judd is a client. Nothing more."

"Of course," she agrees, but I catch the doubt in her voice.

I close my office door and lean against it, my heart pounding despite my carefully maintained composure.

Three months of seeing him multiple times per week. Three months of professional intimacy, working closely together on a project that requires collaboration and trust. Three months of navigating the dynamic that made us click four years ago, the easy partnership that made me believe we could overcome anything.

He claims it's purely business, that the past doesn't matter.

Maybe it is.

Maybe he really is just protecting an investment, ensuring Sterling's anniversary celebration lives up to corporate standards and market expectations.

But Cameron made his priorities clear four years ago when he chose his family's approval over building a future together. I learned that lesson. Rebuilt my life around it. Became stronger because I had to, because the alternative was letting his rejection destroy me.

And if he thinks showing up at my office and arranging

convenient proximity will change anything, he's about to learn exactly what I'm capable of.

I pull out my phone and text Amanda.

ME:

Schedule the Esperanza walkthrough for tomorrow. 2pm. And book the rest of the week solid with vendor meetings—catering, florists, entertainment, rentals. If Mr. Judd wants to be hands-on, let's see how committed he really is to this level of involvement.

Her response comes immediately.

AMANDA:

You're evil. I love it. Consider it done.

I smile for the first time since yesterday's conference room disaster, feeling some of my control return.

Cameron wants involvement? Fine.

He's about to discover that working with me means playing by my rules, maintaining the professional boundaries he claims to want, keeping his focus on business objectives rather than whatever personal agenda might be driving his unusual level of interest.

I didn't build Luminous Events by being passive or accommodating.

And I'm definitely not starting now.

Cameron

My Aston Martin purrs to a stop at the Esperanza Resort's circular drive, the engine noise cutting off to leave only the sound of wind through palm trees and distant ocean waves. Fifteen minutes early—exactly as planned, giving me time to compose myself before seeing Lianne again.

The limestone facade and manicured grounds stretch across fifteen acres of prime Montecito real estate, the kind of understated luxury that whispers rather than shouts. I've played golf here dozens of times, attended charity galas in the ballroom, closed business deals over expensive dinners in their restaurant. But I've never considered it for corporate events, never looked at it through that lens.

Leave it to Lianne to see possibilities I missed, to understand instinctively what spaces can become rather than just what they are.

My phone buzzes.

LIANNE:

> Running 5 minutes late. Erik Andersen,
> Director of Special Events, will meet you in
> the lobby.

I pocket my phone and head inside, my footsteps echoing across marble floors polished to mirror shine. The lobby smells like expensive flowers and old money, the kind of carefully maintained luxury that attracts celebrities and royalty.

"Mr. Judd?"

I turn to find a tall man approaching, late thirties, with an easy smile and the confident bearing of someone who knows his domain. His handshake is firm and professional, his grip suggesting strength without trying to prove anything.

"Erik Andersen. Pleasure to meet you. Lianne speaks highly of your vision for the gala."

Lianne. Not Miss Peralta. First-name basis suggesting familiarity that goes beyond professional courtesy.

"I'm looking forward to seeing what the Esperanza can offer," I reply, keeping my voice neutral despite the irrational spike of something that feels uncomfortably like jealousy.

"Lianne knows our capabilities better than almost anyone," Erik says as we walk toward the ballroom, his tone carrying warmth that's definitely personal. "We've collaborated on several events over the past few years. Eight or nine major celebrations, I think. She has excellent instincts for matching clients with venues, understanding what spaces can deliver beyond surface aesthetics."

Before I can respond—before I can figure out what to say

that won't reveal too much—I hear heels clicking on marble with familiar rhythm.

Lianne crosses the lobby in a navy dress that emphasizes every curve, the fabric moving with her in ways that make my mouth go dry. Her hair is pulled back in a neat bun that showcases the elegant line of her neck, professional but beautiful in ways that hit me harder than any deliberate seduction attempt could.

"Sorry I'm late," she says, not looking particularly apologetic. "Vendor call ran over."

"No problem at all," Erik replies, his demeanor shifting —warmer, more personal, the kind of ease that comes from genuine friendship. "I was just telling Mr. Judd about our collaboration history."

"Erik's one of the best in the business," Lianne says, and I notice how comfortable they are together. How naturally she moves into his space, how easily he responds to her proximity. "If you're doing an event in Santa Barbara or Montecito, you want Erik's team involved."

"Well, I'm hoping to earn that confidence," I say, hearing how the words come out stiff and formal.

"Shall we start with the ballroom?" Erik suggests, gesturing toward ornate double doors.

The Grand Ballroom is spectacular—soaring ceilings with exposed beams, crystal chandeliers that catch afternoon light from floor-to-ceiling windows, polished hardwood floors that frame the golf course beyond. State-of-the-art sound system, professional lighting grid, a stage that could accommodate anything from string quartet to full band.

Everything Sterling Industries needs for an impressive anniversary celebration.

But I barely take that in. Not when I'm distracted watching Lianne and Erik work together.

They move through the space with synchronized efficiency that speaks to extensive collaboration. She points out details that matter for Sterling's needs—sight lines for speeches, flow patterns for networking, acoustic considerations for different entertainment options. He provides technical specifications and logistical capabilities, his responses so quick and intuitive that he's clearly anticipating her questions before she asks them.

They finish each other's sentences. Anticipate concerns. Build on ideas with collaborative energy that makes them look like a well-oiled team.

Like people who've worked together long enough to develop shorthand and mutual respect that goes beyond professional courtesy.

"The acoustics are particularly good for speeches," Lianne says, gesturing toward the platform at the far end. Her movements are graceful, confident, completely in her element. "We could position the podium here for maximum visibility while maintaining intimacy. Natural sight lines from every table, no pillars or blind spots."

"Exactly what I was thinking," Erik agrees, stepping closer to point out the technical booth along the side wall. "We upgraded the sound system last year specifically for events like this. Crystal-clear audio with no feedback issues, mixing board that can handle anything from live band to recorded speeches."

His hand touches her arm briefly as he guides her attention to something near the windows, the contact casual and familiar in ways that make my jaw clench despite my best efforts to stay professional.

The kind of touch that happens between people who've worked together long enough to develop easy intimacy, who trust each other enough not to worry about boundaries or misinterpretation.

I try to focus on the venue specifications, on the details that actually matter for Sterling's event.

I fail spectacularly.

"Our executive chef specializes in contemporary American cuisine with Mediterranean influences," Erik continues, leading us toward the kitchen access. "Perfect for diverse corporate events where you need to appeal to varied palates while maintaining sophistication."

"We'll want to review menu options carefully," I interject, my voice sharper than intended. "Sterling Industries has specific dietary requirements—board members from different cultural backgrounds, religious considerations, allergy concerns."

Erik turns to me, something shifting in his expression. Recognition, maybe, of the tension I'm failing to hide. "Of course. Lianne usually likes to review preliminary options before presenting them to clients, pare down to the strongest choices. Saves everyone time and prevents decision paralysis."

Lianne usually likes.

As if they have an established routine. A working relationship built on mutual understanding and repeated collaboration.

As if this isn't the first time they've done this dance, and it won't be the last.

"I prefer to be involved in all major decisions from the beginning," I say, hearing how it sounds even as the words leave my mouth—controlling, micromanaging, exactly what Lianne accused me of yesterday. "Streamlines the process if everyone's aligned from the start."

Lianne's eyebrows rise slightly, her expression carefully neutral but I catch the flash of irritation. "Mr. Judd prefers a hands-on approach to all aspects of the planning process," she explains to Erik, her voice carrying notes of barely suppressed frustration. "More involved than typical corporate clients."

Erik glances between us, something shifting in his expression as he clearly picks up on undercurrents that have nothing to do with event logistics. His smile turns slightly knowing, understanding dawning. "Most executives at your level delegate event planning to their staff. Trust the professionals they hire to handle details."

"This anniversary is particularly important to Sterling's positioning," I reply, the explanation sounding weak even to my own ears. "Critical moment in our market strategy."

It's a reasonable explanation for hands-on involvement. But even as I say it, I know anyone paying real attention can see there's more to my intense interest than brand management and market positioning.

"Why don't we look at the private dining options?" Lianne suggests, her tone suggesting she's eager to move this tour along. "The board will want exclusive space for pre-event meetings."

As we walk through corridors lined with expensive art and fresh flowers, I watch Erik continue to defer to Lianne's expertise. Asking her opinion on room configurations. Following her lead on discussing capacity and ambiance. Treating her as the primary decision-maker despite my presence as the client's representative.

They've clearly worked together enough times to develop trust and mutual respect. To anticipate each other's needs and preferences. To build the kind of professional partnership that looks effortless but takes years to cultivate.

The kind of partnership that could easily become something more personal, if it hasn't already.

I don't like that thought. Don't like the way it makes my chest tighten, don't like the jealousy creeping through my careful composure.

Which is completely irrational. Lianne is a grown woman who can choose her own colleagues and business relationships. What she does, who she works with, whether she develops friendships or romances with people in her professional circle—none of that is my concern. None of that gives me any right to feel possessive or territorial.

Except it feels like my concern. Feels like watching someone else enjoy the easy partnership we used to have, the collaborative energy that made working together as satisfying as any other aspect of our relationship.

"How long have you two been working together?" I ask before I can stop myself, the question emerging with barely concealed interest.

They exchange a glance I can't read, some private communication passing between them.

"About three years," Erik replies, his tone neutral but his eyes knowing. "Since Lianne started Luminous Events and needed venue partnerships. Eight or nine major events. All successful."

"All successful," Lianne adds, and I catch the pride in her voice. Pride in what they've built together, in their track record of collaboration.

Three years. Enough time to build the kind of rapport I'm witnessing. Enough history to develop connections that go beyond professional courtesy, to create inside jokes and shorthand that excludes outsiders.

Enough time to develop feelings that might not be purely professional.

"Lianne is one of the most talented event planners in the city," Erik says, and there's genuine admiration in his voice that goes beyond colleague praising colleague. "Her ability to understand client needs and translate them into memorable experiences is exceptional. The Esperanza is fortunate to work with her regularly."

The praise is genuine, delivered with respect and what might be fondness. But there's also something else in how he looks at her—appreciation that might be purely professional but feels like it could tip into attraction with the right encouragement.

"I'm sure you appreciate her talents," I reply, my voice cooler than intended, loaded with implications I don't quite mean to convey.

The silence that follows is charged with tension everyone feels but no one acknowledges.

Lianne's eyes narrow slightly, picking up on the undercurrent in my words. "Perhaps we should see the outdoor spaces," she says, her voice taking on a professional crispness that suggests I've crossed some line. "The terrace would be ideal for cocktail hour."

The terrace is spectacular—manicured gardens stretching toward ocean views, strategic lighting that would create ambiance after sunset, heaters for temperature control, sound system for background music. Everything needed for the sophisticated cocktail hour I know Lianne's envisioning.

"Perfect for the pre-dinner reception," Lianne says, moving toward the stone balustrade that overlooks formal gardens. Her movements are graceful and controlled, but I can see tension in her shoulders. "Guests can mingle naturally, enjoy the views, transition smoothly into dinner service."

"The acoustics work well for background music and conversation," Erik adds, positioning himself beside her with the ease of someone who's done this many times before. "We can provide heating if the evening gets cool. Full bar service, passed appetizers, whatever you envision."

Again, working in sync. Again, that collaborative energy that speaks to extensive history together.

I feel myself getting irrationally territorial about a woman who isn't mine, about a relationship that ended four years ago, about professional partnerships that have nothing to do with me.

"Security considerations?" I ask, trying to redirect my focus to legitimate concerns. "Guest access, privacy, crowd control?"

"Fully addressed," Erik replies, his tone suggesting he's handled this question countless times. "Private access from ballroom, controlled entry points, discrete security staff. We've handled high-profile events before—celebrities, politicians, corporate executives requiring privacy and protection."

"What kind of high-profile events?" I press, unable to stop myself from probing for details about their working relationship.

Lianne turns to face me directly, irritation flashing in her dark eyes. "Mr. Judd, if you have concerns about my qualifications or the venue's capabilities, perhaps we should discuss them directly rather than through leading questions that waste everyone's time."

Erik looks between us, clearly recognizing this has ventured into territory that has nothing to do with event logistics. "I'll give you both some time to discuss the details privately," he says diplomatically. "I'll be in my office when you're ready to continue the tour or discuss next steps."

He disappears back into the resort, leaving us alone on the terrace.

"What exactly are you doing?" Lianne demands, her voice low and fierce. "That unprofessional display of—what was that? Jealousy? Territoriality?"

"I'm evaluating a venue," I reply, hearing how weak the excuse sounds.

"No, you're being territorial and unprofessional. Interrogating Erik like he's done something wrong, questioning my vendor relationships with barely concealed suspicion." She steps closer, her eyes blazing. "Erik is one of the most respected event coordinators in the region. If you have a problem with my professional network, say so directly instead of this passive-aggressive performance."

She's right. My behavior has been out of line, crossing from legitimate questions into something that looks like jealous boyfriend rather than professional client.

"I don't have a problem with your vendor choices," I say finally, forcing myself to be honest even though it makes me feel exposed. "I have a problem with..." I stop, struggling to articulate jealousy I have no right to feel.

"With what?" She steps closer, her eyes searching mine. "With the fact that I have professional relationships that don't include you? With the fact that I built a career and a network without your approval or involvement?"

The accusation hits home because it's partially true. Four years ago, I was part of her professional world—attending events together, making introductions, opening doors. Now I'm watching her work with other people, seeing the easy collaboration that used to be ours, the trust and respect she's built with colleagues who actually showed up for her.

"You're right," I admit, my voice rough. "My questions were out of line. Erik seems highly competent and professional."

"He is competent. He's also someone I trust, someone who helped me build Luminous Events when I had more ambition than connections." There's something in her voice —gratitude, respect, maybe more—that makes my chest tight with emotions I'm not ready to name. "Someone who never made me feel like I didn't belong."

The unspoken comparison stings because it's accurate. I made her feel like she didn't belong in my world, like her background was something to hide rather than honor.

"Were you involved?" The question escapes before I can stop it, my voice rough with barely suppressed emotion. "Personally, I mean. With Erik."

Lianne stares at me, her expression shifting from anger to something that might be pity. "That's none of your business. My personal relationships—past, present, or future—are not part of our professional arrangement."

She's right, but her non-answer tells me what I suspected. Something happened between them, even if it's over now. Erik's familiarity with her isn't just professional courtesy—it's built on personal history I wasn't part of.

"You're absolutely right," I say, my voice tight. "I apologize for overstepping professional boundaries. Your personal life is your concern, not mine."

"Good. Now, can we focus on whether this venue meets Sterling's requirements, or do you need to interrogate more of my professional contacts before we can proceed?"

The sarcasm is well-deserved. I've behaved like a jealous boyfriend rather than a professional client, letting personal feelings override business judgment.

"The venue is perfect," I admit, looking around the terrace with genuine appreciation. "Everything Sterling Industries needs—the space, the prestige, the logistical capabilities. Erik's team clearly knows what they're doing."

"Then we'll move forward with the Esperanza?" Her voice is businesslike, but I catch the slight tremor that suggests she's not as composed as she appears.

"Yes. Absolutely."

She makes a note on her iPad, her movements sharp with residual tension. "I'll coordinate the contract details with Erik and have everything ready for your review by next week. Standard terms, cancellation policies, insurance requirements."

"Lianne," I say as she turns to leave, unable to let her go without trying to repair some of the damage. "For what it's worth, you've built something amazing," I say as she turns to face me. "Luminous Events, your reputation, your professional relationships. I'm glad you found your place in this world, that you created success on your own terms."

Something flickers in her expression—surprise, maybe, or confusion—before the mask slides back into place. "Thank you. That means more than you probably realize."

She disappears inside the resort, leaving me alone on the terrace with regrets I can't voice and jealousy I have no right to feel.

I stand there for several minutes, processing the uncomfortable realization that seeing Lianne comfortable with another man bothers me far more than it should. That watching her professional intimacy with Erik triggers possessiveness I haven't felt in years, protective instincts that have no place in our current dynamic.

Four years ago, I let her go because I was too young and too scared to fight for what we had. Too concerned about my family's approval, too worried about social expectations, too cowardly to risk disappointment or confrontation.

I chose the easy path—the one that didn't require me to stand up to my parents or defend Lianne against their judgment. The path that let me keep everyone happy except the one person who actually mattered.

And she moved on. Built a life, a career, relationships that don't include me. Found colleagues who respect her, clients who value her, possibly romantic partners who appreciate her in ways I failed to demonstrate.

She doesn't need me anymore.

She doesn't need my approval, my involvement, or my validation. She's successful, respected, surrounded by people who treat her as an equal rather than a secret to be hidden.

Everything I should want for her, everything I claimed to want when we were together and I talked about supporting her dreams.

Everything I failed to give her when it mattered most.

The realization settles over me like cold water, washing away the irrational jealousy to reveal something harder to face—the understanding that I don't get to be upset about her moving on. I don't get to feel territorial about a woman I pushed away. I don't get to resent the professional and personal connections she built after I proved I wasn't worth her trust.

I gave up that right four years ago.

The question now is whether I can earn it back—not through words or grand gestures, but through consistent action that proves I've actually changed.

Whether I can become someone worthy of a second chance with a woman who's already proven she doesn't need me to be complete.

My phone buzzes with an email from my mother about the Vitale dinner I cancelled, another attempt to orchestrate my personal life according to her preferences. I delete it without reading, the gesture feeling simultaneously satisfying and insufficient.

Small steps. Proving through actions, not words, that I've learned what matters.

Even if Lianne never gives me a second chance, I owe her this. I owe her the man I should have been four years ago—the man who would have fought for her instead of taking the easy way out, who would have made her feel chosen rather than hidden, who would have stood up to family pressure instead of crumbling under its weight.

The man who would have deserved her in the first place.

5

____

Lianne

"You're going to pop that balloon."

I look down to find I've strangled the yellow balloon I'm supposed to be twisting into a fish, the latex stretched thin and ready to burst from my white-knuckled grip. Around me, Highland Community Center buzzes with volunteers transforming the social hall for tomorrow's Filipino-American Friendship celebration. Paper lanterns hang from the ceiling in vibrant reds and golds, tables wait for centerpieces that honor both cultures, and the air smells like sampaguita flowers and fresh paint.

"Sorry," I mutter, loosening my grip and watching the balloon slowly return to its proper shape.

"Uh-huh." Maya Navarro sets down her remarkably accurate balloon parrot—somehow she's managed to create actual feathers and a curved beak—and gives me the look that's gotten the truth out of me for six years. The look that says she knows I'm spiraling and she's not letting it go. "What's going on?"

I should have known she'd notice. Maya has an uncanny ability to read my moods, probably developed during our years of friendship that began in college. We bonded over the challenges of dating men from different worlds, though her story ended better than mine did.

"Just work stuff." I attempt to craft my balloon into something resembling a fish. It looks more like a deformed banana with fins. "The Sterling gala timeline is tight."

"Work stuff that has you checking your phone every five minutes and destroying innocent balloons?" Maya studies my face for a few moments, her brow furrowing. "Oh no. Please tell me this isn't about Cameron."

The balloon deflates with a sad squeak as my grip reflexively tightens.

"How did you—"

"Lianne." Maya's voice carries that particular mix of affection and exasperation reserved for best friends being deliberately obtuse. "You've been weird all week. Distracted during calls, tense at dinner Tuesday, avoiding details about your biggest contract. Cameron is your client, isn't he?"

I nod, abandoning the balloon to the growing pile of my failures. "Board chair. Primary investor. The person who approves every major decision and insists on being involved in ways that go beyond standard client oversight."

"Wow." Maya runs a hand through her dark hair, processing. "When did you find out?"

"Last week. Walked into the pitch meeting expecting Sterling Industries' marketing director, and there he was. Sitting at the head of the table like he belonged there, which I guess he does now."

"That must have been awful."

"It was." I pick up another balloon, this one blue, and start twisting without any clear plan. "But I handled it. Professional boundaries established. No drama. Clear expectations about our working relationship being purely business."

"And how's that working out?"

The question hangs between us, heavier than it should be.

Not well, actually. Because Cameron hasn't contacted me once in seven days since the Esperanza walkthrough, and I'm irrationally annoyed about it despite telling myself I want distance. He promised hands-on involvement, daily check-ins, personal oversight of major decisions. Instead—radio silence except for brief emails routed through his assistant about contract terms and insurance requirements.

Which should be a relief. Should be exactly what I claimed to want when I told him to keep things professional.

It's not.

"He's different than I expected," I admit, my voice barely audible over the community center's ambient noise.

"Different how?"

"More... serious. Focused. Like he actually cares about the work and not just the status it brings." I pause, trying to articulate something I barely understand myself. "He listened during the venue walkthrough. Really listened, not just waiting for his turn to talk or checking his phone while I presented options. Asked thoughtful questions about impact and purpose rather than just aesthetics and cost."

Maya nods, her expression understanding. "Four years is a long time. People change, grow into different versions of themselves. The Cameron you knew at twenty-six might not be the Cameron at thirty."

My phone buzzes. Cameron's name flashes on the screen, sending my heart into an irregular rhythm that's both thrilling and terrifying.

My heart does something complicated—skipping a beat before hammering too fast, my stomach flipping in ways that have nothing to do with hunger or nerves about tomorrow's event.

"Speak of the devil," Maya says, noticing my reaction. "Answer it."

I stare at the phone for another ring, paralyzed by uncertainty. What if it's just business? What if it's something more? What if I hear his voice and all my carefully constructed boundaries crumble?

"Take it," Maya says firmly, her voice brooking no argument. "But remember—you're not the same person you were four years ago. You get to decide what you're worth now. You get to set terms and walk away if they don't work for you."

I answer on the fourth ring, trying to sound calmer than I feel. "Lianne Peralta."

"Miss Peralta." Cameron's voice is warm but maintains formal distance, each word carefully chosen. "I hope I'm not interrupting anything important."

"Just volunteer work. Nothing urgent." I walk toward the corner of the social hall where I can have some privacy, aware of Maya watching me with concerned interest. "What can I do for you?"

"I wanted to discuss the anniversary gala planning," he says, and I notice something in his voice—a tension that suggests he's been thinking about this call, preparing for it.

"Are you free tomorrow afternoon? There's something I'd like to show you related to the event."

I sit up straighter, my balloon-twisting forgotten. A week of silence, and now he wants to meet? "What kind of something?"

"A potential addition to the anniversary celebration. Something that could enhance the event's meaning and impact." His voice is deliberately vague, revealing nothing. "I'd prefer to discuss it in person rather than over phone or email."

Vague. Controlled. Giving me just enough to pique my interest without committing to details that might let me prepare or maintain distance.

"What time?" I ask, my curiosity overriding my better judgment.

"Two o'clock. I'll text you the address." He pauses, and I hear what might be uncertainty in the silence. "And Miss Peralta? I'd appreciate your honest opinion about what I want to show you, not just your professional assessment. This is personal as much as it is business."

The line goes dead before I can respond, leaving me staring at my phone with more questions than answers.

I return to where Maya is working, her balloon parrot now joined by what looks like a remarkably detailed monkey.

"Well?" Maya prompts, not looking up from her creation.

"He wants to meet tomorrow. Says he has something to show me related to the gala." I sink back down beside her, picking up my abandoned fish-banana hybrid. "Something personal."

"Something mysterious that requires an in-person

meeting on a Saturday?" Maya raises an eyebrow, her expression skeptical. "Executives don't do mysterious, Lianne. They do efficient. They schedule conference calls and send detailed agendas and minimize time waste."

She's right. Cameron could have explained over the phone, sent files via email, scheduled a standard meeting at his office or mine with clear objectives and time limits. Instead, he's being deliberately cryptic, creating curiosity that guarantees I'll show up despite my reservations.

"What do you think he wants?" I ask, needing her perspective to cut through my confusion.

"I think he's trying to show you something that can't be explained in an email or demonstrated in a boardroom." Maya picks up her balloon parrot, examining it critically. "The question is—what do you want from him?"

It's the question I've been avoiding all week, the one that keeps me awake at three in the morning when professional defenses are down and honesty feels unavoidable.

"Four years ago, I wanted him to choose me over his family's approval," I say quietly, my voice barely audible over the community center noise. "To fight for us instead of taking the easy way out when his mother made it clear I wasn't suitable for their world."

"And now?"

"Now I don't need his world anymore. I've built my own." I gesture around the community center, at the volunteers creating celebration for a community that matters to me. "I have work I love, friends who accept me completely, a community where I belong without having to prove myself constantly. I don't need Cameron's family's approval or his connections or his money to validate my worth."

"That's not what I asked." Maya's voice is gentle but insistent, cutting through my deflection. "Do you want him to belong in your world now? Or do you still want to belong in his? Because those are very different questions with very different answers."

I stare at the deflated balloon in my hands, at evidence of my inability to create something cohesive when my thoughts are this scattered.

The truth is, I don't know if I want Cameron's world anymore—the country club dinners and charity galas, the careful navigation of social hierarchies and family expectations, the constant awareness that I'm different and that difference matters to people who control access and opportunity. It's one thing to plan them all; it's another to want to be in them.

But I'm starting to suspect I might want Cameron to see mine. To understand what I've built without him, what matters to me beyond professional success and industry recognition. To recognize that I'm not the insecure girl who needed his approval to feel worthy, who let his family's judgment make her feel small.

"I'm scared," I admit, the words emerging before I can stop them.

"I know. But what if you don't let yourself find out?" Maya sets down her balloon creations and takes my hand. "What if you spend the rest of your life wondering what might have happened if you'd been brave enough to see who he's become? To let him see who you've become?"

The next afternoon, I pull up to the address Cameron texted.

It's not Sterling Industries' corporate office. It's not a venue or vendor location or any of the places I'd logically expect for a business meeting about event additions.

It's the LA County Youth Services building in Boyle Heights.

I sit in my car, engine idling, staring at the modest brick building with its colorful murals depicting hope and possibility. Basketball courts behind chain-link fence. Playground equipment that's seen better days but still functional. Signs advertising tutoring programs, job training, college prep services.

This is where foster kids come when they age out of the system. Where teenagers learn to navigate a world that hasn't prepared them for independence, that offers more obstacles than support. Where counselors try to bridge the gap between childhood dependence and adult self-sufficiency, usually with inadequate resources and overwhelming caseloads.

I know because I spent plenty of time here as a teenager, sitting in those same offices, talking to counselors who meant well but couldn't fix systemic problems, attending workshops about job applications and apartment hunting and all the practical skills other kids learn from parents I didn't have.

Cameron's Aston Martin is already parked near the entrance, incongruous among the older sedans and economy cars that suggest staff rather than clients.

What the hell is he doing here?

I walk inside, my heels clicking on linoleum floors that have been cleaned countless times but still show years of wear. The walls are covered with hopeful posters about college scholarships and career opportunities, bright colors trying to compensate for institutional grimness that no amount of optimism can completely hide.

The receptionist directs me to a conference room on the second floor, her smile warm and genuine in ways that suggest she actually cares about the people who walk through these doors.

Through the glass wall, I can see Cameron sitting at a table with three people I don't recognize. He's leaning forward, elbows on the table, listening with complete attention to a woman in a County Services polo shirt. His body language suggests genuine engagement rather than polite interest, his expression serious and focused.

He looks up as I approach, and something in his expression makes my breath catch—vulnerability mixed with hope, nervousness underlying confidence. Like what I'm about to see matters deeply to him and he's terrified of my reaction.

He stands when I enter, his movements betraying tension despite his composed expression. "Miss Peralta. Thank you for coming. I know this is unusual."

"Mr. Judd." I glance at the others, trying to understand what's happening. "What's going on?"

"I'd like you to meet Elena Rodriguez, Director of Youth Services." He gestures to the woman in the polo shirt, who extends her hand with warm professionalism. "Nathan Collins, College Readiness Coordinator." A younger man with glasses nods from across the table. "And Jasmine Williams, who runs the job training program." A woman about my age smiles with genuine welcome.

They shake my hand warmly, their expressions suggesting they know who I am in ways that make my stomach flip with anxiety.

"Cameron has been telling us about a potential partnership," Elena says, her voice carrying enthusiasm that suggests whatever Cameron proposed excited her. "We're very excited about the possibility of what this could mean for our participants."

I look at Cameron, confusion and curiosity warring for dominance. "Partnership?"

He pulls out a chair for me, the gesture both courteous and strategic—positioning me at the table as a participant rather than observer. "Sterling Industries wants to establish a scholarship and mentorship program for foster youth aging out of the system. Specifically targeting kids interested in business, hospitality, event planning—careers where connections and opportunities matter as much as credentials, where family background creates advantages some kids never get."

My heart stops. My breath catches. The room suddenly feels too small and too large simultaneously.

"We'd like to announce it at the anniversary gala," he continues, his voice steady despite my obvious shock. "Make it a central part of Sterling Industries' legacy celebration. Not just looking backward at what we've accomplished, but forward at what we're investing in. Using our platform to create opportunities for kids who deserve them."

I stare at him, unable to process what I'm hearing. This can't be real. Cameron Judd—Pacific Palisades royalty, the man who once worried about what his family would think of my foster care background—is proposing a program specifically designed to help kids like I was.

"Cameron mentioned you might have insights we need," Elena says, pulling my attention from my spiral. "As someone who's been through the system and built a successful career, your perspective would be invaluable in designing a program that actually helps rather than just looking good in press releases. We want to create something meaningful, not just performative."

He told them. He told them about my background, about foster care, about everything I usually keep private in professional settings because revealing that vulnerability invites judgment and assumptions.

And he brought me here to be part of this, to use my experience to shape something that could change lives.

"I..." My voice doesn't work properly, emotion clogging my throat. "I'd need to know more about the structure. What kind of support you're envisioning. How it would work practically."

For the next hour, they walk me through the proposal with detail that suggests extensive planning. Full scholarships for college or vocational training—not just tuition but housing, books, living expenses, everything that keeps talented kids from pursuing education. Paid internships at Sterling Industries and partner companies—real opportunities with mentorship and skill development, not just resume padding. Housing support for kids transitioning out of group homes—bridging the gap between institutional living and independent housing that so many kids fall through.

Mentorship matching with professionals in their chosen fields—not just advice but genuine relationship building, the kind of support that makes difference between surviving and thriving.

It's comprehensive. Thoughtful. Exactly what I wish had existed when I was eighteen and terrified, aging out with nowhere to go and no one to call when things went wrong.

And Cameron sits there, asking intelligent questions, taking detailed notes, deferring to my opinions like they matter more than his wealth or his company's reputation. Listening when I talk about what actually helps versus what looks good on paper. Accepting corrections and suggestions without defensiveness.

"We'll need time to review everything thoroughly," I say finally, my professional mask barely holding against the emotion threatening to overwhelm me. "But this is... it's impressive. More than impressive. It's exactly what these kids need."

"We'd love to have Luminous Events involved in the program design going forward," Nathan says, his enthusiasm evident. "Maybe some of your interns could be program participants? Create pathways from education to employment that don't require family connections."

They're offering me a chance to be part of something that changes lives, that creates opportunities I had to fight for alone.

Because of Cameron.

The meeting wraps up with handshakes and promises to follow up with detailed proposals, timeline discussions, budget considerations. Elena walks us to the elevator, still talking enthusiastically about implementation strategies and partnership possibilities.

When the elevator doors close, leaving Cameron and me

alone in the mirrored cube, I turn on him with emotions I can't name.

"What was that?"

"A partnership proposal between Sterling Industries and LA County Youth Services."

"You told them about me. About foster care. About my background." My voice shakes despite my efforts to control it.

"I told them we'd benefit from consulting someone who understands the system from the inside, who knows what actually helps versus what just sounds good in board presentations." His voice is careful, measured, like he's navigating dangerous territory. "If I overstepped your privacy boundaries—"

"You did overstep." My voice cracks. "But why? Why this program, why now, why bring me into it?"

The elevator reaches the ground floor but Cameron doesn't move to exit, just holds the door open button so we can finish this conversation.

"Because you were right," he says quietly. "Four years ago, you said I had privilege and responsibility. That people with resources should use them for something that matters beyond accumulating more wealth. That success without purpose is just empty accumulation."

He pauses, and I see something raw in his expression. "I didn't listen then. I was too focused on maintaining what I had, on not disappointing my family, on taking the path of least resistance. But I'm listening now."

The sincerity in his voice breaks something in my chest, cracks open defenses I've spent four years building.

"This isn't just about the gala," I say.

"No. It's not."

"Then what is it about?"

"It's about becoming the man who deserves a second chance," he says. "Even if I never get one. Even if you decide I'm four years too late and the damage is permanent."

The elevator doors start to close. Cameron catches them, holding them open while I process what he's saying.

"You don't have to be involved if this makes you uncomfortable," he continues. "If bringing up your past or asking you to share that experience feels exploitative, I'll find other consultants. But I wanted you to know that I'm not just saying I've changed. I'm proving it. I'm using the privilege you called me out for having to create opportunities for kids who deserve them."

As he steps out of the elevator, I want to tell him that he's four years too late. Still, he's trying and I have to give him that.

I follow him out, my legs shaky, my heart pounding. He's standing near the entrance, backlit by afternoon sun streaming through the doors, looking uncertain in ways I've never seen from him.

"Cameron," I say as he turns to face me. "I want to be involved. In the program. I want to help design something that actually works, that creates real pathways rather than just good publicity."

Relief washes over his face, transforming his expression. "Thank you. That means more than you know."

"But I need to understand something." I step closer, needing to see his eyes when he answers. "If this just about the gala, what is this really about?"

"It's about honoring what you taught me," he says simply.

"About becoming someone worthy of your respect, even if I never earn back your trust or your love."

For the next few moments, I don't know what to say. I don't know how to process this version of him who listens and acts and uses his privilege for purposes beyond self-interest.

So I just nod, accepting his words without committing to anything beyond professional involvement.

But as I walk to my car, I can feel something shifting. Some wall crumbling that I thought was permanent.

Maybe people can change. Maybe four years is enough time to learn hard lessons and become different versions of ourselves.

And maybe second chances aren't always mistakes.

6

———

Cameron

THE STAIRS of my Gulfstream fold down at Van Nuys Airport, California sunshine hitting me like a wall after twelve hours in pressurized darkness. Forty-eight hours touring German solar facilities—meetings with engineers, site visits to production plants, negotiations that required precision even through jet lag. Twelve-hour flight with turbulence over the Atlantic that made sleep impossible despite the leather seats and expensive whiskey.

I should go straight home. Shower off the travel grime, sleep for ten hours in my own bed, give my body time to adjust to the eight-hour time difference.

Instead, I tell my driver to take me to Luminous Events.

Because waiting another week to see Lianne isn't an option my self-control can handle. Because I've spent forty-eight hours thinking about her while pretending to focus on renewable energy infrastructure. Because jet lag makes me honest in ways sobriety and adequate sleep might prevent.

"Mr. Judd, welcome back," Amanda says as I step into the

lobby, her expression shifting from professional greeting to concern when she sees me properly. "How was Europe?"

"Productive." I manage a smile that probably looks as exhausted as I feel. "Is Miss Peralta available? I know I don't have an appointment, but I was hoping to catch up on planning progress."

Amanda's eyes take in my rumpled suit, the shadow of beard I didn't have time to shave, the way I'm gripping my briefcase like it's the only thing keeping me upright.

"She's in the conference room reviewing floral samples," Amanda says. "I'll bring coffee—you look like you need it."

She's not wrong. I've been surviving on airplane coffee and determination for the past twenty-four hours.

Through the glass walls, I can see Lianne arranging flower samples on the conference table. She's wearing a burgundy dress that makes my jet-lagged brain forget how to form coherent thoughts, the color perfect against her brown skin. Her hair is down today, falling past her shoulders in waves that catch afternoon light.

She looks up as I approach, and for just a moment, before professional composure clicks into place, I see genuine concern flash across her features.

"Mr. Judd." She stands, setting down the white rose she was examining. "How was your trip? You look..."

"Like I need sleep?" I settle into a chair, grateful to sit after what feels like days on my feet. "The negotiations went well. Long but successful."

"That's good." She gestures to the arrangements spread across the table, a rainbow of options that probably mean something to her trained eye but just look like flowers to my exhausted brain. "I've put together several options for centerpieces. Each represents a different aesthetic approach for the gala."

I try to focus on what she's showing me, to engage with the careful planning she's clearly invested hours into. Roses, lilies, orchids, each arranged with artistry that would be impressive if I could concentrate properly.

They're all beautiful and completely interchangeable in my current mental state.

"These are excellent," I say, my voice rougher than intended. "You've covered the full range of possibilities. Very thorough."

Lianne studies my face, her expression shifting from professional presentation to something softer. "Cameron, when did you last sleep?"

The use of my first name catches me off guard, a slip in her careful formality that reveals concern she's trying to hide.

"On the plane. Sort of." I rub my eyes, trying to clear the grit and exhaustion. "Turbulence made it difficult."

"You should have rescheduled this meeting. Gone home to rest." There's something in her voice—genuine worry beneath professional courtesy. "These decisions can wait until you're actually conscious enough to make informed choices."

"I wanted to see you." The words slip out before jet lag can censor them, too honest and too revealing.

Lianne's breath catches, her eyes widening slightly before she looks away. "The flowers?"

"You," I clarify, because apparently exhaustion strips away my filter completely. "I wanted to see you, Lianne. To hear your voice. To be in the same room with you instead of halfway around the world thinking about you during business meetings."

The silence that follows pulses with tension, with everything we're not saying, with admissions neither of us is ready to fully acknowledge.

"The roses represent traditional corporate elegance," Lianne says finally, moving beside the white and cream blooms with deliberate focus. "Classic, sophisticated, appropriate for Sterling Industries' established reputation and fifty-year history."

I nod, trying to follow her shift back to business despite my heart pounding at her proximity. She smells like jasmine and something citrusy, a scent that's uniquely hers and makes my exhausted brain want to close the distance between us.

"The orchids are more contemporary," she continues, her voice carefully neutral. "Modern, innovative, forward-thinking. They represent evolution and adaptation—appropriate for a company expanding into renewable energy and new markets."

She's good at this. Even exhausted, I can appreciate the strategy behind each choice. Lianne doesn't just arrange flowers—she creates narratives, tells stories through design that resonate with deeper meaning.

"What about peonies?" I ask as Lianne freezes, her hand hovering over an orchid arrangement.

"What about them?"

They're your favorite flowers, although you could never allow yourself to enjoy them because they're expensive, not local, I almost say out loud but I don't.

"They're elegant. Sophisticated." I'm improvising now,

trying to justify a suggestion that came from four-year-old memories rather than aesthetic judgment. "Soft colors, interesting texture. Romantic without being obvious about it."

"Peonies." Her voice is carefully neutral, but I catch the slight tremor. "They're beautiful flowers. Very expensive this time of year—out of season, which means importing from specialized growers."

She pauses, her fingers unconsciously touching a rose petal. "Are you sure that's what you want for the centerpieces?"

"Some things are worth the extra cost," I say, meeting her eyes. "Some things are worth going out of season for, worth the logistics and expense and complication."

"Cameron," she begins, then stops. Her hand reaches toward mine on the table, hovering in the space between us like a question neither of us knows how to answer. "I think we should focus on practical options that serve Sterling's needs rather than personal preferences."

She's giving me an out. A chance to step back from the edge we're approaching, to maintain the professional boundaries we've both claimed to want.

I should take it. Should agree that roses are more appropriate, that peonies are too expensive and too complicated and carry too much personal meaning for a corporate celebration.

"You're right," I say finally, forcing myself to choose practicality over sentiment. "The roses. Traditional arrangement. That's the right choice for Sterling's brand positioning."

Safe. Practical. No emotional baggage or complicated history.

Lianne nods, making notes with movements that are too

brisk, too controlled. The tension in her shoulders wasn't there before my suggestion.

"I'll coordinate with the florist to ensure adequate supply," she says, her voice professionally neutral despite the emotion I can see in the set of her jaw. "White roses with gold accents, traditional arrangement style."

"Is there anything else you'd like to review today?"

I fight back a yawn, my body finally registering the exhaustion I've been pushing through. Lianne notices immediately, her expression softening despite her obvious effort to maintain professional distance.

"You don't have to be doing this personally, you know," she says quietly. "Reviewing floral arrangements while you can barely keep your eyes open? Most executives delegate these decisions to their staff, trust the professionals they hire to handle details without micromanagement."

She's giving me another out. A graceful way to step back from the involvement that's forced us together, that's made maintaining boundaries increasingly difficult.

"I want to be here," I say, more honestly than intended, the jet lag stripping away careful pretense. "Not because I don't trust your judgment—you're the best at what you do, everyone knows that. But I want to be part of creating something meaningful. I want to understand your vision, to see how you transform concepts into reality."

I pause, meeting her eyes despite the exhaustion threatening to pull me under. "I want to work with you, Lianne. To be your partner in this, not just your client."

Lianne searches my face. "Who are we now?"

"I don't know," I admit. "But I'm enjoying finding out. Even when I'm too tired to think straight, even when it's complicated, even when it means examining why I suggested peonies when we both know roses are more appropriate."

Lianne's breath catches. For a moment, I think she might say something that changes everything, that acknowledges what's building between us despite our best efforts to maintain professional distance.

Instead, she looks down at her notes. "I think we've covered everything for today. I'll have the final floral specifications by tomorrow, along with updated timeline documentation. And we have the wine vendor meeting in Santa Barbara on Thursday."

It's a dismissal. Polite but firm, creating distance even as something in her voice suggests she doesn't entirely want me to leave.

Though Santa Barbara means time alone with Lianne away from the careful boundaries of offices and conference rooms. Even if she insisted we drive separately, even if she's maintaining professional formality, it's still hours we'll spend together outside our usual context.

"Of course," I agree, standing despite my body's protest. "Thank you for accommodating my schedule despite the lack of advance notice."

"It's what we do for our clients," she says, but there's something in her tone that suggests I'm not just another client. That maybe, despite everything, she's as affected by this proximity as I am.

I'm halfway to the door when she speaks again.

"Cameron."

I turn back, surprised by my first name rather than formal title.

She's standing by the conference table, one hand resting on the surface, her expression caught between concern and something softer. "Get some sleep. You look like you need it."

"I will," I promise, meaning it. "Thank you."

"Good." She seems to catch herself, her formal mask back on. "Sterling Industries needs you at full capacity for the final planning phase. Can't have the board chair making decisions while sleep-deprived."

Sterling Industries. Right. Because this is about business, about ensuring their event succeeds, not about her caring whether I'm taking care of myself.

"Of course. Have a good evening, Lianne."

"You too, Cameron."

I leave with her name on my lips and peonies in my head, with the memory of her concern warming something in my chest despite the exhaustion pulling at my limbs.

Somewhere between the jet lag and the flowers, I cracked open a door that's been closed for four years. Let slip admissions I meant to keep contained, revealed feelings I'm supposed to be managing better.

I just hope I'm strong enough to walk through it when the time comes.

And that she'll be brave enough to let me.

7

—————

Lianne

"Vehicle system error. Please contact service immediately."

The red warning glows from my Tesla's touchscreen, mocking me. I tap the screen, jab the key fob, but the dashboard stares back with digital indifference.

Perfect. Wine vendor meetings in Santa Barbara in three hours, Amanda's using our other vehicle for a wedding, and my backup options are vanishing.

Footsteps echo across the parking garage.

"Car trouble?"

Cameron walks toward me from the elevator, looking unfairly good in dark jeans and a navy button-down despite the early hour. His hair is slightly mussed in a way that stirs memories I've been suppressing.

"Good morning," I say, scrambling for why he's here. "I thought we were meeting at the venue."

"I figured I'd catch you before you left." His eyes take in

my dead dashboard. "I wanted to discuss the wine selections." He pauses. "I could drive, if that would help."

Two to three hours in a car with Cameron. Just the two of us. Confined in a space the size of a luxury closet.

Either the best idea I've heard all week or a complete disaster.

"That's generous," I say carefully, "but I'm sure you have better things to do than chauffeur event planners around wine country."

"I'm the board chair of Sterling Industries. Part of my job is ensuring our gala exceeds expectations." He says it like it's obvious. "If that means driving to Santa Barbara to select wine pairings, that's what I'll do."

"This would be strictly business," I say, more to myself than him.

"Absolutely. Nothing but professional wine evaluation."

There's something in his tone that makes me look at him more carefully, but his expression is perfectly serious.

"Alright," I decide, ignoring the voice screaming this is a terrible idea. "I appreciate it."

He grins. "Excellent."

Twenty minutes later, I'm sinking into the passenger seat of Cameron's Aston Martin, leather seats impossibly soft and luxurious.

"Comfortable?" he asks, adjusting the climate control.

"Very." Though comfortable doesn't cover what I'm feeling. The car is beautiful, but what's making me nervous is the forced intimacy of sharing this small space with Cameron for the next few hours.

"Music preferences?" His finger hovers over the controls.

"Whatever you usually listen to is fine."

Cameron scrolls through an extensive playlist, settling on something that makes me sit up straighter.

"The Lumineers?" I recognize the opening notes of a song I haven't heard in years. "I wouldn't have expected that from someone with season tickets to the LA Philharmonic."

"I have varied tastes." He pulls into morning traffic. "Besides, you used to love this album. I figured there was a chance you still did."

The casual reference catches me off guard. I'd forgotten Cameron knew I loved folk music, that we used to argue good-naturedly about indie bands versus classical composers.

"You remember that?"

"I remember a lot of things," he says quietly, then catches himself. "This song came up on my playlist a few weeks ago. Brought back memories."

The song fills the space between us, familiar and bittersweet. We used to listen to music like this during long drives to venues, debating lyrics and sharing discoveries.

"So, about your Europe trip," I say, needing safer territory. "Renewable energy, right?"

Cameron navigates onto the 101 with ease, and I catch myself staring at his hand on the gear selector—the same strong fingers I used to trace during our drives together, back when touching him felt as natural as breathing.

"Acquisition deal in Copenhagen and Frankfurt," he replies as I tear my gaze away. "We're expanding into renewable energy infrastructure."

"That's different from your usual investments."

I remember his interests being more traditional—real

estate, tech companies, established industries with predictable returns.

"Very different. Two years ago, I wouldn't have touched anything so volatile." He glances at me briefly. "But sometimes the most meaningful investments are the ones that feel risky."

There's something in how he says it that makes me think he's not just talking about business, but I focus on the gray clouds gathering over the mountains instead.

"Looks like we might be driving into weather."

"Should clear by afternoon," Cameron says, glancing at the darkening sky. "We have three wineries today?"

"For a 50th anniversary, we need multiple producers. Different styles, different price points, options for various courses." I make mental notes about timing. "With the compressed schedule, we need to finalize everything today. No second chances."

"Right, the three-month timeline." Understanding crosses his face. "That's why today is so packed."

He returns to our earlier conversation as we pass a produce truck heading toward Santa Barbara's agricultural regions.

"I realized that playing it safe all the time means missing opportunities that could actually matter. I was so focused on maintaining what I had, protecting established returns, that I stopped looking for ways to make real impact."

"And renewable energy makes real impact?"

"It should. If we do it right—partner with communities instead of just extracting resources, think about long-term sustainability instead of quarterly profits." He pauses. "I've been learning that the most profitable ventures often serve purposes beyond making money."

It's a more thoughtful philosophy than the Cameron I knew four years ago, who seemed focused on building wealth and maintaining family approval. This version asks different questions about success and meaning.

"That's actually impressive," I admit. "Most people in your position don't look beyond traditional strategies."

"Most people in my position are smarter than I was at twenty-six." His smile is self-deprecating. "It took me a while to figure out that having money isn't the same as having purpose."

The conversation flows easily as we drive through Ventura County's rolling hills. Cameron tells me about renewable projects, and I find myself genuinely interested in his strategic thinking. He asks thoughtful questions about Luminous Events' growth, about balancing creativity and commerce.

It's the kind of conversation we used to have during those long venue visits, talking for hours about vision and strategy. But there's a depth to Cameron's thinking now that wasn't there before, a consideration for impact and sustainability that suggests he's learned to see beyond immediate returns.

"What about you?" he asks as we pass through Carpinteria. "What's changed for you?"

I consider the question, watching the coastline come into view.

"I learned that I don't need anyone's permission to belong in spaces where I create value," I say finally. "Four years ago, I was always trying to prove I deserved to be in the room. Now I know I deserve to be there because I'm good at what I do."

"You were always good at what you did," Cameron says quietly. "Even four years ago. I just wasn't mature enough to recognize how good."

The admission catches me off guard—partly because it's more honest than I expected, partly because it addresses something I didn't realize I needed to hear.

"You were twenty-six," I offer him grace. "We were both figuring things out."

"Maybe. But you were figuring out how to build something meaningful. I was figuring out how to avoid disappointing people who probably shouldn't have had so much influence over my decisions."

It's the closest he's come to acknowledging what really happened between us, why he ended things so abruptly.

Part of me wants to push for details, to finally understand the calculations that led him to choose his family over what we were building.

But another part—the part enjoying this conversation, this glimpse of who he's become—doesn't want to ruin the moment by bringing up the past.

"Well," I say instead, "it sounds like we've both learned some things."

"Yeah," he agrees, and when he glances at me there's something warm and hopeful in his expression. "I think we have."

The playlist shuffles to another song I recognize, something Cameron introduced me to during our relationship. Without thinking, I start humming along, then catch myself and stop.

"Don't stop," Cameron says. "You always had a beautiful voice."

Heat creeps up my neck. He's right—I do love to sing, and I used to sing constantly when we were together. Such a small detail, but the fact that he remembers makes something flutter in my chest.

"You remember that, too?"

"I remember you singing in my kitchen while you cooked." His voice takes on a softer quality. "Humming in the car during long drives. I remember thinking that hearing you sing was one of my favorite sounds."

The memory hits unexpectedly—lazy Sunday mornings, road trips to venues, quiet moments when it felt like we had all the time in the world.

"You used to play piano," I find myself saying. "Do you still?"

"Sometimes. When I can't sleep or when I'm working through complicated problems." He adjusts his grip on the wheel. "Music helps me think."

"What do you play when you can't sleep?"

"Chopin, usually. Something complicated enough to require focus but familiar enough that I don't have to think about the mechanics."

I smile, remembering how he used to play late at night when stressed about work or family. "Nocturne in E-flat major?"

"You remember that?"

"You played it the night before your sister's wedding. You were worried about your speech."

Cameron laughs, genuine and surprised. "I can't believe

you remember. I was terrified I'd embarrass Sophia in front of three hundred guests."

"You were perfect. Your speech was beautiful." The memory is vivid and bittersweet. "You talked about love being worth fighting for, about choosing the person who makes you want to be better. It was one of the most romantic things I'd ever heard."

The silence that follows pulses with contradiction. We both know the irony—Cameron giving a speech about fighting for love months before he chose the easier path of family approval.

"I meant every word of that speech," he says quietly. "I just wasn't brave enough to live up to it."

For a moment, I'm tempted to push him to explain more —what his family said, what threats or promises convinced him to walk away.

Instead, I hear myself say, "We were young. People change. What matters is who we are now."

Cameron glances at me. "Who are we now?" he asks, before turning his attention back on the road.

"I don't know," I admit. "But I'm enjoying finding out."

The admission slips out before I can stop it, more honest than I intended.

But it's true.

Sitting in this car, listening to music that reminds us both of better times, talking about growth and change and who we've learned to become—it feels easy in a way I didn't expect.

Natural.

Right.

Dangerous.

Cameron reaches across the console. His hand hovers near mine on the armrest, close enough that I can feel the warmth of his skin, far enough that I could pull away if I wanted.

I don't pull away.

His fingers brush mine, the lightest touch, a question more than a claim.

My breath catches. Four years since he touched me, and my body still remembers—still responds like no time has passed at all.

"Lianne," he says, my name barely more than a whisper.

The GPS interrupts with directions to the first winery, and the moment shatters.

I pull my hand back, creating distance even as my skin protests the loss of contact.

"We should focus," I say, my voice unsteady. "Professional wine evaluation, remember?"

Cameron's jaw tightens, but he nods. "Right. Professional."

But even as we suddenly busy ourselves with the world around us, him on the road ahead and me with the landscape, we both know something shifted in that almost-touch.

And there's no taking it back.

8

———

Cameron

"This is exactly what we need for the cocktail reception."

I watch Lianne make notes about the Sauvignon Blanc we've just tasted, her professional focus impressive despite being two wineries and several samples into a longer day than either of us anticipated.

Storm clouds that looked manageable this morning have developed into something more ominous, but neither of us has suggested cutting the day short.

We're at our second winery, a boutique operation in the hills above Santa Barbara that specializes in small-batch wines. Lianne has been taking detailed notes at each location, asking technical questions, keeping everything strictly professional despite the increasingly relaxed atmosphere that comes with spending hours tasting wine together.

"The minerality works well with the appetizer menu we discussed," she continues, swirling pale liquid with practiced ease. "Light enough not to compete with food, complex enough to keep people interested."

I nod, though I'm more interested in watching her work than evaluating mineral content.

There's something mesmerizing about how Lianne approaches these tastings—methodical but passionate, analytical but intuitive. She tastes each wine like she's having a conversation with it, understanding its personality before deciding how it fits into the larger story she's creating.

"You're good at this," I observe.

"It's part of the job," she replies, a faint blush coloring her cheeks.

"No, it's more than that. You understand how wine works with food, with atmosphere, with the overall experience. Most event planners just pick whatever's in budget."

Lianne looks at me with something like surprise. "You've been to a lot of corporate events."

"Too many. Most of them are exercises in expensive mediocrity." I take another sip. "This is different. You're creating something that will actually enhance the evening instead of just filling glasses."

"That's the goal," she says, smiling.

An hour later, storm clouds darken to charcoal gray as we drive to our final stop, weather reports getting more urgent.

"One more stop," Lianne says, checking her notes. "The Esperanza Resort's wine cellar. They have an exclusive partnership with a local vintner."

The Esperanza. Where we had our awkward venue walkthrough, where I behaved like a jealous idiot about Erik.

"Straightforward tasting," Lianne continues as rain begins to fall against the window in heavy drops. "Their reserve wines are supposed to be exceptional."

At the Esperanza, the wine cellar is exactly what I'd expect from a property frequented by billionaires who collect vintage bottles like art. Stone walls, temperature-controlled storage, intimate seating areas designed for exclusive tastings.

Frederick de Vries, the resort's sommelier, greets us with professional warmth despite the storm outside. He's prepared five wines, each paired with small bites demonstrating how flavors work together.

"We'll start with our signature Chardonnay," he explains, pouring pale gold liquid into crystal glasses.

The wine is exceptional—complex and elegant. But what captures my attention is watching Lianne's reaction. Her eyes close briefly as she tastes, a small smile playing at her lips.

"This is incredible," she says, making detailed notes. "The balance between oak and fruit is perfect."

As the tasting progresses, I find myself paying less attention to wines and more to Lianne. The way she asks thoughtful questions. The way she considers how each wine will work with different courses. The way her professional expertise shines through every interaction.

But I also notice other things. The way she laughs more easily as the afternoon progresses. The way she meets my eyes when she finds a wine particularly impressive. The way the formal distance we've maintained all week has gradually dissolved into something more comfortable.

More natural.

"For our final selection," Frederick says, leading us deeper into the cellar, "I'd like you to try something special. This Cabernet is from a very limited production—only fifty cases made. It's not available for purchase, but the Esperanza occasionally offers it for special events."

He leads us to a private tasting alcove carved into stone foundation. Small table, two chairs positioned close together. Soft lighting from actual candles rather than electric fixtures.

Intimate.

"I'll give you privacy to evaluate this properly," Frederick says, pouring deep-red wine into our glasses. "Take your time. This wine deserves careful consideration."

He disappears, leaving us alone in what feels like a cave designed for romance.

"This is beautiful," Lianne says, looking around. "I had no idea this space existed."

"Private tastings for special clients, probably." Though I'm more interested in how candlelight catches highlights in her dark hair.

She takes a sip and her expression becomes almost reverent. "Cameron, you have to try this. It's extraordinary."

I taste the wine—exceptional, with layers that reveal themselves gradually. But watching Lianne's face as she savors it is more intoxicating than any wine.

"We have to include this," she says excitedly. "I know it's exclusive, but for Sterling Industries' 50th anniversary..."

"Whatever you think is best," I agree, though I'm not thinking about the gala anymore.

For a moment she's quiet as rain hits the windows above us and thunder rolls in the distance.

"Listen to that storm," Lianne says, glancing upward. "We might be here longer than planned."

"Would that be so terrible?" The question comes out before I can think better of it.

She looks at me, wine glass still in hand, a thoughtful expression on her face. "Cameron…"

"I know," I say quietly. "This is supposed to be business."

"It is business." But her voice lacks conviction, and she doesn't move away when I set down my wine glass and turn to face her fully.

"Is it? Because sitting here with you, watching you work, listening to you laugh—it doesn't feel like business anymore."

Outside, the storm builds. Inside our private alcove, everything feels suspended. Waiting.

"We agreed to keep things professional," Lianne says.

"We did. And I've tried. God, I've tried." I reach out to touch her hand where it rests on the small table. "But I can't pretend I don't feel this. Whatever this is between us."

She doesn't pull away. Instead, she looks down at where our fingers have intertwined, her breath catching.

"This is complicated," she whispers.

"I know."

"We have history. Bad history."

"We do. But we also have this." I gesture between us, encompassing the wine-warmed intimacy, the way we've spent the day rediscovering each other. "And I don't want to pretend it doesn't exist anymore."

Lianne lifts her gaze to meet mine. "Cameron…"

"Just this once," I say softly, moving closer. "Let me show you who I am now. Not who I was four years ago, but who I've become."

For a moment, I think she's going to pull away, retreat behind professional boundaries.

Instead, she whispers, "This is a mistake."

But she doesn't move.

"Probably," I agree, cupping her face in my hand, thumb brushing across her cheekbone. "But I'm tired of making the safe choice."

The kiss starts soft, tentative. A question more than a statement.

But when she responds—when her lips part under mine and she makes a small sound of surrender—everything else falls away.

I kiss her like I'm memorizing the moment, like I'm trying to communicate everything I've learned about love and regret and second chances since the day I let her go.

She kisses me back with the same urgency, her hands tangling in my hair, and I forget we're sitting in a wine cellar. I forget our entire history is built on pain.

All I can think about is this moment. The way her body fits against mine like it was meant to be there. The way her breathing quickens as I deepen the kiss. The way she shivers when I touch her.

Time stands still, the storm outside forgotten as we explore each other, rediscovering old scars and new desires in flickering candlelight.

When we finally break apart, both breathing hard, the storm has intensified. Rain pounds against windows, thunder crashing closer.

"That was..." She trails off, uncertain how to finish.

"A mistake?" I suggest, half-joking.

Because God knows it probably is. But it also feels like the most natural thing in the world, like four years of regret and longing have led us here.

"Not a mistake," she says, shaking her head. "Just... complicated."

I can't argue with that. There's still so much we haven't talked about, so many questions left unanswered.

But right now, all I want is to kiss her again.

So I lean in slowly, giving her time to pull away.

She doesn't. She leans in too, and when our lips meet this time, there's no hesitation. We both know what we want.

The second kiss is even better than the first. When I slide my hand into her hair, Lianne sighs against my mouth, a sound that makes my heart skip.

Thunder rumbles overhead. She pulls away slightly.

"Shit. The storm..." she whispers, tucking a stray lock behind her ear.

"Getting worse," I agree, though I'm not focused on weather.

She looks up at me, lips wine-dark and kiss-swollen, eyes wide with something that looks like wonder mixed with fear.

"What happens now?" she asks quietly.

Before I can answer, Frederick appears at the alcove entrance, expression apologetic but urgent.

"I'm sorry to interrupt, but I wanted to let you know—the storm has intensified significantly. Highway patrol is advising against travel on coastal routes." He pauses. "The roads are becoming dangerous. You might want to consider waiting it out here, or finding accommodation nearby."

The mention of staying cuts through our wine-warmed intimacy.

Lianne glances at me, then at the windows where rain streams down in sheets.

"We should probably head back before it gets worse," she says, standing. "Beat the worst of it."

I want to argue. Want to suggest we stay, find a room, continue what we started in this candlelit alcove.

But the uncertainty in her eyes tells me she's not ready for that. This kiss was a huge step for her. For both of us, after everything that's happened. Pushing for more would be pushing too hard.

"You're right," I say, standing. "We should go."

Frederick looks doubtful. "Are you certain? The conditions—"

"We'll be fine," I assure him, though I'm already regretting the decision.

As we gather our notes and head toward the exit, I can hear rain pattering steadily against windows, wind picking up. What looked manageable from inside the cellar seems heavier now.

"Doesn't look too bad," Lianne says, checking her phone for weather updates. "Maybe we can beat the worst of it."

I look at her, still feeling the warmth of her lips, still processing what just happened between us.

"Should be fine once we get on the freeway," I agree, though I'm more focused on the fact that we'll have another ninety minutes alone in the car together.

Ninety minutes to figure out what this kiss means.

Ninety minutes to navigate whatever this is becoming between us.

She nods, pulling her jacket on. "Let's go before it gets worse."

As we step out into the storm, rain immediately soaking us, I realize that "worse" might not be about the weather at all.

It might be about what happens when we can't pretend this is just business anymore.

9

Lianne

I stare through the windshield at endless red brake lights stretching down the 101. At least we made it to the highway all the way to Ventura. But what had lessened as light drizzle just minutes earlier is back to a steady downpour and traffic hasn't moved in twenty minutes.

"Weather reports are saying multiple accidents," Cameron says, checking his phone. "Overturned cargo truck near Oxnard. They're recommending people avoid this stretch entirely."

The rain pounds harder. Several cars ahead have their hazards on. A few brave souls are pulling over to the shoulder, giving up.

"We could be here for hours," I say, trying not to think about what that means. Alone in this car, with the memory of our wine cellar kiss still fresh between us, nowhere to go.

"There's an exit coming up." Cameron points to a barely

visible sign. "Ventura. We could get off, wait it out somewhere."

I consider our options. Sit in traffic for an unknown amount of time, or exit into a small coastal town where accommodation options will be limited at best.

Neither feels particularly safe.

"How long do you think this will last?"

Cameron checks the radar. "Storm system is moving slowly. Could be several more hours before conditions improve."

Several more hours. Together.

After everything that happened in that wine cellar.

"Ventura it is," I decide, because sitting in gridlocked traffic in the middle of a storm feels worse than whatever awkwardness awaits us in a hotel room.

The Ventura Harbor Inn is a modest two-story building that looks like it was built in the seventies and updated in the nineties. Not the Ritz-Carlton, but clean and well-maintained, with a surprisingly full parking lot.

"Lot of other people had the same idea," I observe.

"Storm refugees," Cameron agrees.

The lobby is crowded with weather-displaced travelers. Families with restless children, business travelers checking phones, couples huddled over coffee.

The desk clerk—a tired-looking woman in her fifties—greets us with the expression of someone who's dealt with this chaos all evening.

"Let me guess. Freeway closure?"

"Traffic jam from hell," Cameron confirms. "Do you have any availability?"

She consults her computer with slow deliberation. "I have one room left. King bed, ocean view. It's our honeymoon suite, actually, but under the circumstances..."

"Do you have two rooms available?" I ask quickly, heat creeping up my neck.

She shakes her head. "I'm sorry, that's all I have. The storm has everyone stranded. You're lucky I have anything at all."

I look at Cameron, unsure.

One room means sharing space, sharing the aftermath of that wine cellar kiss, navigating whatever this is between us without separate doors to retreat behind.

"We'll take it," Cameron says, pulling out his credit card.

Twenty minutes later, after a stop at the gift shop where I bought an oversized Ventura T-shirt and basic toiletries, I'm standing in a room clearly designed for romance.

Rose-colored walls. A massive king bed with too many decorative pillows. Floor-to-ceiling windows that would showcase ocean views but currently reveal only rain-streaked darkness.

"Well," Cameron says, closing the door behind us. "This is..."

"Awkward?"

"I was going to say cozy, but awkward works too."

There's one bed. One very large, very obvious bed that makes it impossible to pretend this is just a business arrangement between colleagues caught in bad weather.

"I can sleep on the floor," Cameron offers.

"Don't be ridiculous. It's a king bed. We can share it like adults." The words come out more confident than I feel. "We're both exhausted. We can handle sharing space for one night."

The silence that follows is loaded with everything we're not saying.

That kiss in the cellar. The way he looked at me like I was air.

"If you're sure," he says finally.

"I'm sure."

An hour later, we've both changed into makeshift pajamas—Cameron in a California T-shirt, me in my Ventura shirt that falls to mid-thigh, face scrubbed clean of makeup for the first time since he's seen me again.

I catch him watching me as I pad barefoot across the carpet.

"What?"

"Nothing," he says quietly. "You just... you look like you again."

"Like me again?"

"Like the Lianne I remember. Without all the..." He gestures vaguely. "The armor."

I touch my bare cheek self-consciously. "I look twelve without makeup."

"You look beautiful," he says simply, the honesty in his voice making something flutter in my chest.

He turns out the light, plunging us into semi-darkness. I

can hear rain pounding against windows, punctuated by occasional thunder.

It feels like we're alone in the world.

"So," I say finally, because the silence is unbearable. "This is nice."

Cameron turns his head, amusement in his expression. "The storm? The traffic jam? Or the honeymoon suite?"

"All of it, obviously. Exactly how I planned to spend my Wednesday evening."

He laughs, warm and familiar in the darkness. "Not what I expected when I offered to drive you to Santa Barbara."

"No?" I turn on my side to face him. "What did you think would happen?"

Cameron mirrors my position, and suddenly we're much closer. Close enough that I can see gold flecks in his eyes, close enough that I remember how good he smelled in that wine cellar.

"Honestly? I thought we'd select some wines, maintain professional boundaries, and drive back to LA with a better understanding of Sterling Industries' beverage requirements."

"Very practical."

"I'm a practical man."

But there's something in his voice that suggests he's not feeling particularly practical right now.

"Are you?" I ask softly. "Because kissing me in that wine cellar didn't seem very practical."

The mention of our kiss changes the atmosphere immediately. The careful distance feels suddenly inadequate.

"No," Cameron admits. "That wasn't practical at all."

"Do you regret it?"

He's quiet for so long I start to think he won't answer. When he finally speaks, his voice is rough with honesty and want.

"I regret that it took me four years to do it again."

My breath catches.

"Cameron..."

He reaches out to touch my face, thumb brushing across my cheekbone the same way he did in the wine cellar.

"I've missed hearing you say my name like that," he says quietly.

"I've missed saying it."

When he kisses me this time, it's different from the wine cellar. Less tentative. More certain. Like he knows who I am and wants me anyway.

His fingers slide into my hair, and I make a small sound of surrender as I kiss him back, letting go of the past, letting go of everything but this moment.

Cameron pulls me closer, and I can feel the heat of his body, the hardness of him against my hip. My hands find the hem of his shirt, fingers skating across bare skin, feeling the muscles of his abdomen tense under my touch.

"Lianne," he breathes against my mouth, his hands exploring the curve of my waist, sliding up my ribcage. "God, I've missed you."

I've missed you. The words he didn't say in the wine cellar. The words that have been unspoken since that conference room.

"I've missed you too," I admit, because I don't have energy to pretend anymore.

His mouth moves to my neck, finding that spot below my ear he somehow still remembers, and I gasp, arching into him. My oversized T-shirt has ridden up, and his hand finds bare skin at my hip, fingers tracing patterns that make me shiver.

"You're so beautiful," he murmurs against my throat. "Every part of you."

When his hand slides higher, cupping my breast through the thin cotton, I moan softly, pressing into his palm. This is what I've been missing, what I've been denying myself—this feeling of being completely wanted, completely seen.

He kisses me deeper, his tongue sliding against mine, and I respond with equal hunger, my hands fisting in his shirt to pull him closer. We're a tangle of limbs and desperate touches, four years of longing compressed into frantic kisses and wandering hands.

Cameron rolls us over so he's above me, settling between my legs, and I can feel all of him—his weight, his heat, the hard length of him pressing against me through our clothes.

"Cam," I whisper, and he kisses me again, slower this time, more deliberate.

His hand finds the hem of my shirt, fingers tracing the bare skin of my stomach, moving higher. I arch into his touch, wanting more, wanting everything.

But then reality crashes over me like cold water.

This is Cameron. The man who chose his family over me. The man who broke my heart so completely that I spent four years building walls to protect myself.

And I'm about to let him in again. I'm about to give him everything, risk everything, after one day of wine tasting and car conversations.

I pull away abruptly, pressing my hands against his chest.

"I can't," I whisper, fighting back tears. "I can't do this."

Cameron freezes, his eyes searching my face in the darkness. "Lianne—"

"I'm sorry." My voice breaks. "I just... I can't."

He rolls off me immediately, giving me space, his breathing as ragged as mine.

"Don't apologize," he says quietly. "You have nothing to apologize for."

I sit up, hugging my knees to my chest, trying to calm my racing heart. "I want to. God, Cameron, I want to. But I'm terrified."

"Of what?"

"Of you," I admit. "Of this. Of believing in us again and having it fall apart like it did before."

Cameron sits up too, careful not to touch me but close enough that I can feel his presence.

"Because I'll hurt you again," he says, understanding in his voice. "Because four years ago I chose them over you, and you can't survive that happening again."

The fact that he gets it—that he understands exactly what I'm afraid of—makes the tears fall.

"I believed in you once," I whisper. "I believed in us. I let myself think that love could overcome everything—family pressure, social expectations, the casual cruelties of people who thought I didn't belong in your world." I look at him. "And you let me down."

Cameron's hand comes up to cup my face, his thumb brushing away tears. "I was twenty-six and terrified of disappointing anyone. I chose wrong, Lianne. I chose fear over you, and I've regretted it every day since."

"But what's different now? Your family still won't approve. The same obstacles—"

"The difference is that I don't care about their approval anymore." His voice is raw with honesty. "I've spent four years building something independent of them, proving to myself that I don't need their money or their blessing to succeed. The only approval that matters to me now is yours."

I search his face for any sign of the uncertainty that destroyed us before. All I see is determination and something that looks like love.

"I'm scared," I admit.

"So am I," he says. "But I'd rather be scared with you than safe without you."

I lean my forehead against his, closing my eyes. "I need time. I need to know this is real, that you won't run when things get hard."

"I'll give you all the time you need," Cameron promises. "I'll wait as long as it takes."

When he kisses me again, it's gentle. Reverent. A promise instead of a demand.

"Just hold me?" I ask quietly. "Can we just... hold each other tonight?"

"Yeah," he says, pulling me down beside him, wrapping his arms around me. "We can do that."

I settle against his chest, listening to his heartbeat, feeling the rise and fall of his breathing. His hand strokes my hair, soothing and patient.

"Thank you," I whisper. "For understanding."

"Thank you for being honest," he replies. "For telling me what you need."

Outside, the storm continues to rage. But inside our rose-colored sanctuary, wrapped in Cameron's arms, I feel safe enough to close my eyes.

Safe enough to imagine a future where this might actually work.

Safe enough to hope.

10

Cameron

I WAKE to sunlight streaming through the honeymoon suite's floor-to-ceiling windows and an empty bed beside me.

The sheets where Lianne slept are still warm, her scent lingering on the pillow, but she's gone. For a moment I lie still, processing the absence and what it might mean. Last night was everything and nothing—we kissed with desperate urgency, held each other like drowning people finding shore, fell asleep wrapped together in ways my body remembered even after four years of separation.

But she pulled back before we could go further, and waking up alone sends a familiar chill through me that feels like history repeating.

I pull on yesterday's clothes and head downstairs, following the scent of coffee and the sounds of quiet conversation to the hotel's breakfast area.

I find Lianne at a corner table, already dressed in yesterday's navy dress and her hair pulled back in a neat bun. She's nursing a steaming cup of coffee while looking at her phone.

"Good morning," I say, settling across from her even though part of me wonders if she wants me to keep my distance.

She looks up, and I catch fleeting softness before her professional mask slides into place.

"Good morning. You were sleeping so peacefully I didn't want to wake you." Her cheeks flush pink as she looks away. "I thought I'd grab coffee and check road conditions while you rested."

"Thank you," I say, meaning it. "How long have you been up?"

"About an hour. Couldn't sleep." She pushes another cup of coffee across the table towards me. "Highway patrol cleared the accidents overnight. Traffic should be manageable if we leave soon."

"Busy day?"

"I have client meetings this afternoon," she replies, not meeting my eyes. "So we should head back to LA as soon as possible. Get back to our respective responsibilities."

Client meetings. Right back to careful distance, as if last night never happened. As if we didn't fall asleep in each other's arms after the most honest conversation we've had in four years.

"Of course," I say, accepting the coffee she prepared and trying not to read too much into the gesture. "Whatever works best for your schedule."

Twenty minutes later, we're back on the road. The morning is clear and bright, last night's storm leaving everything washed clean and sparkling. But the atmosphere in my car feels heavy with everything we're not saying, with the distance Lianne is trying to recreate after last night's intimacy.

"So," I say as we merge onto the 101, desperate to fill the silence. "Last night was…"

"Professional," Lianne cuts me off, not looking up from her laptop balanced on her knees. "We shared accommodations out of necessity due to weather conditions. Very… businesslike."

Businesslike. Right. After everything that happened—the kiss, the tears, falling asleep wrapped around each other—she's going to pretend it was just a practical arrangement.

"Speaking of professional matters," she continues, cheeks slightly pink despite her controlled tone, "I've been thinking about your suggestion for the centerpieces."

It takes me a moment to remember through my frustration. "The peonies?"

"I think they'd work beautifully for the private dining room where board members will have their pre-dinner meeting." She finally glances at me, expression carefully controlled. "More intimate than the main ballroom, but still elegant. Personal without being obviously romantic." She pauses. "If that's what you want."

"Yes," I say, probably with more intensity than floral arrangements warrant. "That's definitely what I want."

Lianne's breath catches slightly at something in my tone, but she immediately returns to her laptop. "Good. I'll confirm with the florist today."

"Good."

"The wine deliveries need coordinating with venue staff. I'll work with Jennifer on final counts and service timing," she says, her attention on her phone as if she's reading a list. "We should have everything locked in by next week."

Next week. When this project moves into final execution phase and our interactions become less frequent. When we'll both be too busy managing logistics to spend long days tasting wine and pretending we don't remember what it felt like to fall asleep in each other's arms.

"Sounds good," I manage, though nothing about this sounds good. Nothing about returning to professional distance and careful boundaries feels right after last night's honesty.

The easy banter dies, replaced by silence that feels more forced with each passing mile. Lianne buries herself in work, responding to emails and coordinating with vendors with the focused intensity of someone who needs distraction from uncomfortable thoughts.

I focus on traffic and try not to think about how right she felt in my arms last night. How beautiful she looked when she finally let her guard down. How much I want to pull over and kiss her until she stops pretending last night didn't mean anything.

By the time I pull up to her office building, we've successfully reestablished the client-vendor relationship we both apparently want to maintain. Professional. Distant. Safe.

Everything I hate.

"Thank you for the ride, Cameron," she says, gathering her things. "And for... handling the accommodation situation professionally last night."

"Lianne—"

"I'll send over the updated timeline by end of day," she continues, cutting off whatever I was going to say. "The floral specifications, wine delivery coordination, everything you need for your review."

She's out of the car before I can respond, disappearing into her building with quick steps that suggest she's fleeing rather than simply returning to work.

I sit in my car for several minutes after she's gone, processing what just happened and what it means.

She's scared, just like she told me last night. Terrified of trusting me again, of believing that this time could be different. So scared that she's retreating into professionalism as armor against feelings she doesn't want to acknowledge.

And I totally get it.

After what I did four years ago, she has every right to protect herself.

Too bad understanding doesn't make it hurt less.

The drive from downtown LA to my Malibu home takes forty-five minutes through morning traffic—enough time to process what just happened between Lianne and me and figure out how to move forward without pushing her away completely.

By the time I pull into my circular driveway, I've almost convinced myself that maintaining professional boundaries is the smart choice for both of us. That respecting her need for distance is the right thing to do.

Then I see the cars parked in front of my house, and every good intention evaporates.

My father's silver Mercedes. My mother's white Range Rover. And a red Ferrari I don't recognize.

Great. Just great.

I sit in my car for a long moment, gathering energy to deal with whatever family situation is waiting inside. It's barely noon on Saturday, which means this is either crisis intervention or another attempt at orchestrated social obligation I'm supposed to accept gracefully.

Given the Ferrari, I'm betting on the latter.

I'm halfway to my front door when it opens to reveal my mother, dressed in country club brunch attire and wearing the kind of smile that suggests she's up to something.

"Cameron, darling," she says, air-kissing my cheek with practiced efficiency. "We were beginning to worry. James said you didn't come home last night."

Of course James told them. My housekeeper has been reporting my comings and goings to my mother since I was in high school, probably because she thinks parental oversight is appropriate regardless of age.

"Business trip," I say, technically true. "Wine vendor meetings in Santa Barbara that ran late due to weather."

"You're handling wine vendor meetings personally?" My father appears behind her, wearing his weekend uniform of expensive polo and pressed slacks, his expression skeptical. "That seems unusually thorough for a board chair with global responsibilities."

Before I can deflect, a third person emerges from my house—blonde, beautiful in white linen, moving with the unconscious grace of someone who's never doubted her place in any room.

"Cameron, it's been forever," Isabella Vitale says, extending a manicured hand. "Your parents have told me so much about what you've been up to since Milan."

I shake her hand and summon social training drilled into

me since childhood, the polite charm that comes automatically even when I want to be anywhere else. "Welcome to Los Angeles. How are you finding it after Milan?"

"Different, but charming in its own way. Your parents have been wonderful hosts, showing me around." Her smile is genuine, her demeanor friendly without being overly familiar.

"We were just heading to the club for brunch," my mother says, her tone making it clear this is not really a request. "Isabella's parents are meeting us there. You should join us, darling."

Translation: Isabella's parents—Charles and Patricia Vitale, major players in international fashion and luxury goods, business connections spanning three continents—are joining us, and this is an opportunity I'm expected to appreciate and leverage.

"I should probably shower and change," I say, looking at my rumpled clothes that smell like hotel soap and hint at exactly how I spent my night.

"Nonsense," my father says with false heartiness. "You look fine. Besides, Charles and Patricia are eager to meet you. We've been discussing potential partnerships for a possible European expansion."

Of course they have. Because this was never about Isabella's fashion career or friendly reconnection—it's about strategic alliances, business opportunities, creating connections that benefit both families.

"Fine," I say, recognizing I'm not winning this battle. "Give me twenty minutes."

Twenty minutes later, I'm in the passenger seat of my father's Mercedes, following my mother and Isabella toward

Pacific Palisades Country Club. The conversation is carefully neutral—questions about Germany, comments about renewable energy trends, observations about California's drought and its impact on landscaping.

What my father doesn't say is more revealing than what he does: why Isabella happens to be in town, why they're all at my house on a Saturday morning, why this brunch somehow requires my presence despite my obvious exhaustion.

"Isabella seems lovely," my father says casually as we navigate winding roads toward the club. "Accomplished, well-educated, excellent family connections in European markets we're targeting."

"Mmm," I reply noncommittally.

"Her father's fashion empire has been expanding into sustainable luxury goods. Very forward-thinking approach to environmental responsibility. Could be valuable partnerships for Sterling's brand positioning."

"Possibly."

"Your mother thinks you two would get along well. Similar backgrounds, shared interests in art and culture. She understands the demands of high-level business relationships."

I glance at him, wondering if he actually believes shared backgrounds and business connections are sufficient foundations for relationships, or if he's just following my mother's script.

"Dad, I'm not looking for anyone to set me up with right now."

"Of course not. Just a friendly introduction. No pressure." But we both know there's always pressure when my parents arrange friendly introductions with eligible daughters of business associates. "She's only in town for a few weeks, thought it would be good to reconnect."

The country club sits on perfectly manicured grounds overlooking the ocean, expensive cars filling the parking lot, members dressed in casual luxury that costs more than most people's wardrobes. I've been a member since eighteen, attended countless events here, played golf with clients on courses where my father taught me that business networking disguises itself as leisure.

The Vitales are exactly what I remember from childhood European vacations. Charles is tall and distinguished with bearing that comes from generations of inherited wealth. Patricia has understated elegance suggesting a lifetime of shopping at places that don't advertise prices, where sales associates know your name and preferences before you walk in.

"Cameron, my boy, how long has it been?" Charles stands to shake my hand, his grip firm without being aggressive. "Your parents speak highly of your business acumen. Sterling Industries' expansion into renewables is quite impressive."

For the next hour, we discuss everything except the obvious reason for this gathering—European fashion trends, sustainable business practices, investment opportunities in emerging markets, renewable energy infrastructure.

Isabella is exactly the kind of woman my parents think I should be interested in—beautiful, accomplished, from the right background with the right connections. She's smart and articulate, asking intelligent questions about Sterling's strategy, sharing insights about fashion industry sustainability initiatives that actually show thoughtfulness rather than just surface knowledge.

She's also nothing like Lianne.

The realization hits me somewhere between mimosas and discussion of Italian manufacturing. Isabella is lovely, but I'm just not interested. When she laughs, it's polite rather than genuine. When she asks about my interests, it feels like interview questions checking boxes. When she touches my arm making a point, it's calculated rather than instinctive.

Everything that should work on paper—shared background, compatible social circles, family approval, business synergies—feels hollow in practice when compared to the electric connection I feel with Lianne. The way Lianne challenges me rather than accommodates me. The way her laugh sounds genuine and unguarded when something truly amuses her. The way she touches me without calculation, driven by feeling rather than strategy.

"Cameron?"

I look up to find Declan Pierce approaching our table, offering a welcome disruption to the awkward family tableau. "Declan. Good to see you."

"You too." He glances at the assembled group with barely concealed amusement. "How's the gala planning coming along?"

"Everything's on schedule," I reply, grateful for the subject change. "We have an excellent event planner handling the details. Very thorough, very professional in handling the compressed timeline."

"That's crucial for these milestone celebrations," he says. "Maya and I just went through planning one of our events for Highland Community Center. The right planner makes all the difference."

Maya. Lianne's best friend. The woman who somehow managed to navigate a relationship with a billionaire developer despite coming from completely different worlds.

"I'd love to hear how that went," I say. "Maybe grab coffee sometime. Compare notes on event planning challenges."

And maybe learn how he and Maya made their relationship work despite obstacles similar to what Lianne and I face.

"I'd like that."

We exchange contact information and a few more pleasantries before Declan excuses himself. The brunch winds down with polite conversation about staying in touch, vague promises about future meetings, the kind of social lubrication that keeps networks functioning.

As we walk back to the parking lot, Isabella on her phone with her assistant coordinating something in Italian, my mother falls into step beside me with the purposeful stride of someone about to deliver a prepared speech.

"She's lovely, don't you think?"

"She seems very nice."

"Very accomplished. Well-connected internationally. Her family's businesses could open significant doors for Sterling's European expansion."

"Definitely well-connected."

"Your father thinks there could be significant business opportunities through closer relationship with the Vitales. Strategic partnerships that benefit both families."

I stop walking and turn to face her directly. "Mother, are we talking about business opportunities or something else?"

Her expression becomes more serious, the social mask slipping slightly to reveal genuine concern. "I'm talking about your future, Cameron. You're thirty. Most men in your position have established more... personal commitments by now. Built families, created stability beyond just business success."

Personal commitments. Such a careful euphemism for marriage, for the kind of strategic partnership she's been trying to orchestrate since I turned twenty-five.

"I'm focused on building Sterling into something meaningful. Creating real impact rather than just accumulating wealth."

"You can do both. Your father managed quite well to build his career while maintaining family obligations and social connections." She pauses, studying my face. "Or is there something you're not telling us? Someone you're being... selective about?"

"No," I lie, because explaining my complicated feelings about Lianne would require conversations I'm not ready to have. There's also the fact that I'm her client. "I just think compatibility matters more than business connections. That relationships should be built on genuine connection rather than strategic advantage."

"Of course it does. But they're not mutually exclusive, darling." Her voice softens slightly. "I just want you to be happy. To find someone who understands your world and can be a real partner in all aspects of your life."

Someone who understands your world. Code for someone from my world, someone who doesn't require explanation or accommodation, someone whose background matches expectations.

In her mind, someone who isn't Lianne.

"I'll keep that in mind," I tell my mother, the words feeling hollow.

After she drives off with Isabella—they're meeting Patricia for shopping in Beverly Hills, apparently—my father and I head back toward Malibu in silence that stretches uncomfortably.

"Isabella seems lovely," he says eventually, breaking the quiet.

"She is."

"Your mother has high hopes for that connection. Thinks you two would be well-matched."

I watch the Pacific glimmer between estates, perfect and distant and unreachable. "Mother has high hopes for a lot of things that aren't going to happen."

"You aren't even going to give it a chance? Get to know her better?"

"I'd rather let things happen organically. Meet people on my own terms rather than through orchestrated introductions designed to produce specific outcomes."

My father's hands tighten slightly on the steering wheel. "Your mother only wants what's best for you. Wants you to find someone suitable who can share your life without complicating it unnecessarily."

The word "suitable" hits like it always does—a reminder that some people are deemed appropriate while others, no matter how talented or accomplished, will never quite measure up to arbitrary standards of background and breeding.

"I'll find my own way, Dad. Make my own choices about who I spend my life with."

We drive the rest of the way in silence, but I can feel his disappointment radiating in the space between us.

When I finally get home, close the door on family expectations and strategic introductions, I pull out my phone and look at the text conversation with Lianne. Her last message from this morning, sent while I was trapped at brunch:

LIANNE:

Floral specs attached. Let me know if you need any adjustments.

Professional. Distant. Safe.

Everything I don't want.

I start typing a response, then delete it. Start again. Delete again.

What do I say? That I spent the morning with exactly the kind of woman my family wants for me and all I could think about was her? That Isabella Vitale is beautiful and accomplished and everything that should work on paper but made me feel nothing?

That last night, holding Lianne in my arms, felt more right than any strategic partnership ever could?

Finally, I just type:

ME:

Specs look perfect. Thank you. Hope you're having a good day.

It's inadequate. Doesn't say anything I actually want to say. But it's all I can manage right now, when I'm exhausted and confused and still processing that my family will never understand why Lianne matters more than all their careful strategic planning.

Her response comes thirty minutes later:

LIANNE:

You too.

Two words. Barely an acknowledgment.

But she responded, which means she's thinking about me too.

It's not much. But right now, it's enough to give me hope that maybe, eventually, we'll find our way back to each other.

Lianne

"Amanda, can you handle the Sterling check-in today?"

I don't look up from my laptop, trying to make it sound casual rather than the careful avoidance it is.

Two weeks.

Fourteen days since I woke up in that hotel room next to Cameron, since we spent an awkward breakfast pretending we hadn't kissed and held each other with desperate tenderness, since I decided that maintaining professional boundaries was more important than exploring whatever this is between us.

Fourteen days of successfully avoiding direct contact, and I'm starting to think I might pull this off.

"Of course," Amanda replies, making a note. "What should I tell him if he asks about timeline adjustments?"

"Tell him we're on schedule. Venue locked, catering confirmed, entertainment booked. Everything's proceeding according to plan."

Which is true. The Sterling Industries anniversary gala is

shaping up to be exactly the kind of sophisticated celebration that will cement Luminous Events' reputation in the luxury corporate market.

The Esperanza ballroom will be transformed into an elegant showcase. The wine selections from Santa Barbara have been delivered and stored. Even the peonies—those expensive flowers Cameron suggested because he remembered they were my favorites—have been confirmed.

I should be thrilled about the professional success. Instead, I find myself checking my phone every few hours, wondering if Cameron will insist on speaking with me directly.

He hasn't.

He's been perfectly professional, accepting Amanda's updates and approving decisions through email and scheduled calls that happen when I'm conveniently in other meetings.

It's exactly what I wanted.

So why does it feel like disappointment?

Maybe it's because of what Maya mentioned last week— something Declan had said about seeing Cameron at the country club with a beautiful blond woman.

"Probably nothing," Maya had added quickly. "You know how these business networking things go."

But the comment lodged itself in my chest like a splinter. A reminder that Cameron moves in circles where beautiful, accomplished women are common. A reminder that whatever happened between us doesn't give me any claim on him.

"Lianne?" Amanda's voice cuts through my brooding. "The Martinez wedding rehearsal is this afternoon. Do you want me to handle the Sterling call before or after?"

"After. Maria deserves my full attention today."

The Martinez wedding is exactly the kind of event that reminds me why I love this business. A celebration of love that's been two years in the planning, with family traditions woven throughout. Maria is a teacher from East LA, Carlos works in construction, and they've saved three years for their dream wedding.

It's the kind of love story that makes me believe in happily ever after.

Even when my own love life feels like a series of complicated mistakes.

"I'm heading out," Amanda calls at six o'clock. "The Sterling call went well. Mr. Judd approved the final entertainment lineup and confirmed the guest count. Five hundred confirmed attendees."

"Great. Did he have questions about the timeline?"

"Just one. He wanted to confirm that you'll be personally overseeing event setup." Amanda pauses, studying my face. "I told him yes. That's standard for premium events."

"Right. Standard."

"He also asked..." Amanda hesitates. "He asked if you were satisfied with how everything was progressing. If there was anything you needed from him."

"What did you tell him?"

"That you're extremely thorough and everything is under control. Which is true." Amanda gathers her things, pausing at my door. "Is everything okay between you and Mr. Judd? The dynamic seems different since Santa Barbara."

Different. Of course it's different.

"Everything's fine," I reply, forcing a smile. "We're focused on delivering an exceptional event."

Amanda nods, though she's not entirely convinced. "Okay. Don't stay too late."

The office grows quiet after she leaves. Just the hum of air conditioning and distant traffic below.

I should go home, order takeout, stream something mindless. Instead, I find myself reorganizing files that don't need organizing, reviewing perfect timelines, doing anything to avoid going home to my empty apartment where I'll have nothing to distract me from the memory of waking up next to him.

The Sterling Industries folder sits on my desk, thick with contracts and vendor agreements. Everything is perfect. The venue, catering, entertainment, flowers. Even the wine selections from that day when Cameron and I rediscovered each other.

The only thing missing is the easy collaboration we had before everything got complicated by hotel rooms and the realization that some feelings never really go away.

I'm so absorbed in unnecessary busy work that I don't hear the elevator or footsteps.

I don't realize I have company until a familiar voice says my name.

"Lianne."

Cameron stands in my office doorway wearing a charcoal suit that emphasizes his broad shoulders, hair slightly mussed as if he's been running his hands through it. There's something in his expression that makes my pulse spike.

He looks tired. Not physically exhausted, but emotionally drained in a way I recognize because I've been feeling the same way for two weeks.

"I thought Amanda handled your call."

"She did." He steps inside, closing the door with a soft click that makes the space feel very small and very private. "But I needed to speak with you directly."

"About what? Everything's on schedule."

He moves closer, not stopping until he's standing in front of my desk. Close enough that I can smell his cologne. Close enough that I'm reminded of how it felt to wake up pressed against his chest.

"It's not about the timeline."

My mouth goes dry. "Cameron..."

"Do you know how long two weeks is, Lianne?"

The question catches me off guard. Partly because it's not what I expected, partly because I know exactly how long two weeks is when you're trying not to think about someone.

"Fourteen days," I answer automatically.

"Three hundred and thirty-six hours." His voice is lower now, more intimate. "Twenty thousand, one hundred and sixty minutes of trying to convince myself that what happened between us didn't matter."

Has he been counting time the same way I have?

I stand, needing distance. "Cameron, we agreed—"

"We agreed to maintain professional boundaries," he says, moving around my desk before I can retreat. "But avoiding me for two weeks hasn't changed the fact that I can still feel you in my arms. That I still remember how it felt to fall asleep with you."

He's right, and I hate that he's right. Two weeks of careful distance crumbling in a single conversation.

"This is complicated," I whisper.

"I know it's complicated." Cameron reaches out to touch my face, thumb brushing across my cheekbone. "But I've missed you. Not just working with you. I've missed the way you laugh. The way you challenge me. The way you feel when you're sleeping against my chest."

The admission breaks something open. Because despite everything—despite the blond at the country club, despite our different worlds, despite all the logical reasons—I've missed him too.

"I've missed you too," I confess. "But that doesn't change anything. We can't—"

"Then stop avoiding me," he says, stepping closer. "Stop pretending that what we shared meant nothing."

I reach up to touch his face, fingers tracing the line of his jaw. "I've been going crazy these past two weeks. Trying not to think about you, trying to convince myself that Santa Barbara was just proximity and wine and bad weather."

"And what conclusion did you reach?"

"That I'm a terrible liar."

Cameron's smile is soft and triumphant. "Good. Because I was starting to think I was the only one losing my mind."

When he kisses me, there's nothing tentative about it. This is two weeks of pent-up longing pouring out in the space between one heartbeat and the next.

I respond immediately, hands fisting in his jacket to pull him closer, body melting against his like I've been waiting for this moment.

The kiss is desperate and hungry, fueled by two weeks of missing each other and pretending we didn't. Cameron's hands are in my hair, at my waist, running down my back like he's trying to memorize every curve.

"God, I've missed this," he murmurs against my mouth.

"Me too," I breathe, then kiss him harder.

We're pressed against my desk now, my laptop pushed aside. His mouth moves to my neck, and I arch against him with a soft gasp that makes him groan.

This is madness. We're in my office, anyone could walk in. I don't care about anything except the way Cameron's hands feel, the way he whispers my name against my skin.

I pull his mouth back to mine, kissing him with an intensity that surprises us both. His response is immediate and overwhelming, hands tangling in my hair, body pressing closer.

We're so absorbed in each other that we almost miss the sound of the elevator, the jangle of keys.

I break away abruptly, both of us breathing hard as voices get closer.

"The cleaning staff," I whisper, scrambling to put distance between us.

Cameron runs a hand through his hair, trying to restore professional appearance, though his kiss-swollen lips make it clear what we've been doing.

"Good evening, Miss Peralta," comes a cheerful voice from the hallway.

"Good evening, Rosa," I call back, hoping my voice sounds normal.

We stand in my office, breathing hard, staring at each other. The interrupted moment hangs between us like an unfinished sentence.

"We should..." I begin.

"Yeah," Cameron agrees, though he doesn't move toward the door.

The spell is broken, but barely. I can still feel the ghost of his hands on my skin, still taste him on my lips. Two weeks of distance undone in ten minutes.

"This is... complicated," I mutter. "Very complicated."

"But not going away."

I look at him—really look at him—taking in his mussed hair and intense eyes and the way he's looking at me like I'm the most important thing in his world.

"No," I admit quietly. "It's not going away."

The cleaning crew's voices get closer, and Cameron straightens his tie.

"I should go," he says, though he doesn't sound like he wants to.

"Probably."

"But Lianne?"

"Yeah?"

"I'm done pretending this isn't real. I'm done avoiding what's between us because it's complicated." His voice is firm, determined. "Two weeks was long enough."

Before I can respond, he's walking toward my door, leaving me standing by my desk with kiss-swollen lips and the lingering scent of his cologne and the absolute certainty that everything between us just changed.

Again.

12

Cameron

Three days after kissing Lianne in her office and I'm struggling to focus on McNeal and Morgan as they discuss Sterling Industries' expansion into renewable energy infrastructure over business dinner.

"The strategic partnerships we're proposing would position Sterling as the primary developer in three key markets," McNeal says, gesturing to the tablet between us. "But the real opportunity is in the regulatory landscape. With the new federal incentives, we're looking at unprecedented growth potential in emergency battery storage."

I nod, making what I hope are appropriate responses about market positioning and competitive advantages. I read their report before the meeting—twice, actually—so I know the material inside and out. The Nevada solar farm has strong fundamentals. The Arizona facility offers excellent ROI projections. The partnership framework they've proposed is actually quite brilliant.

But I can't focus.

This isn't like me. In business settings, I'm known for my laser focus, for asking the questions that cut straight to the heart of what matters. I've closed billion-dollar deals because I never let personal distractions interfere with professional opportunities. My father used to say that my greatest asset was my ability to compartmentalize—to set aside everything else when money and strategy were on the table.

But nothing about my mental state has been normal since Lianne walked back into my life six weeks ago. Since I showed up at her office three days ago and kissed her with the desperation of someone who's been pretending not to want her. Since she kissed me back with the same hunger, the same need, the same acknowledgment that whatever this is between us isn't going away.

And she feels the same way. I know she does. I heard it in her voice when she admitted she'd missed me. I felt it in the way she pulled me closer instead of pushing me away. I saw it in her eyes when the cleaning crew interrupted us and we had to pretend we were discussing floral arrangements instead of tearing each other's clothes off.

So why aren't we taking this further? Why are we letting fear and professional boundaries and four years of hurt feelings keep us apart when we both know we want the same thing?

"Cameron?" McNeal's voice cuts through my distraction, patient but with an edge that suggests this isn't the first time he's tried to get my attention. "What do you think about the timeline for the Nevada project?"

"Sorry," I say, setting down my wine glass and clearing my throat. "Could you repeat the question?"

Morgan and McNeal exchange a glance that's carefully neutral but speaks volumes. They're wondering if I'm actually interested in this partnership or if I'm wasting their time.

"The Nevada solar farm," McNeal repeats, his tone still professional but slightly strained. "We're looking at an eighteen-month development timeline from permitting to operation, assuming no regulatory delays and no policy reversals from Washington."

"Eighteen months seems realistic if we front-load the permitting process," I agree, forcing myself to engage with the details. "What's your contingency plan if the federal incentives change before completion?"

It's a good question—the kind I should have asked twenty minutes ago instead of letting my mind wander to Lianne's office and the way her hair felt tangled in my fingers.

McNeal visibly relaxes, launching into an explanation of their hedging strategy and alternative funding mechanisms. I listen, I nod, I ask follow-up questions that demonstrate I actually understand the complexities of renewable energy development.

But I'm calculating something entirely different in the back of my mind. Eighteen months. That's how long this project will take from start to finish. Eighteen months of meetings and site visits and strategic planning sessions.

And I can't even make it through one dinner without thinking about Lianne.

"Let's review the preliminary timelines then," McNeal says, pulling up detailed charts on his tablet and angling it so I can see. "If we can secure the Nevada permits by Q2, we could break ground by—"

Suddenly my world tilts sideways the moment I catch sight of a familiar figure on the restaurant patio across the promenade, and every word McNeal is saying dissolves into white noise.

Lianne.

She's sitting at a table on the outdoor terrace of the Italian place directly across from us, separated only by the pedestrian walkway that connects this cluster of upscale restaurants. The evening is warm enough that most establishments have their patios full, and I can see her clearly through the glass partition that separates our climate-controlled dining room from the promenade.

She's with Maya Navarro—I recognize her from Declan's social media posts—and a man I recognize as Elliot Walker, the current CEO of Pierce Enterprises and Declan's best friend.

Lianne looks beautiful in a black dress that hugs her curves, her hair loose around her shoulders in a way I rarely see during business meetings. She's laughing at something Elliot and Maya said, her head thrown back with genuine amusement, no trace of the professional mask she wears when we're discussing Sterling Industries' anniversary celebration.

This is Lianne in her natural environment—not the polished event planner managing corporate celebrations with military precision, but the woman who enjoys good food and better company, who lets her guard down with people she cares about.

The woman I fell in love with four years ago.

"I'm sorry, could we take a brief break?" I ask, setting my napkin on the table. "I need to handle something quickly."

As I get up from the table, both men follow my gaze across the promenade, their expressions shifting from confusion to understanding to something that might be amusement.

"It'll only take a few minutes."

"Take all the time you need," McNeal says, a knowing look on his face as I walk away from the table, not caring that walking across the promenade to say hello to my event planner would be unprofessional at best, completely inappropriate at worst.

But I can't stop looking at her. Can't stop thinking about that kiss in her office three days ago, about the way she admitted she'd missed me too, about the promise in her voice when she said she was done pretending this wasn't real.

I want to hear that promise again. I want to see if she still means it.

I walk through our restaurant and out onto the promenade that's busy with evening diners and tourists, the kind of upscale outdoor dining district that makes Los Angeles feel almost European on warm nights like this. String lights create a warm glow overhead, and the sound of conversation and clinking glasses fills the air, mixing with the distant hum of traffic and the occasional burst of laughter from nearby tables.

"Excuse me," I say as I reach their table, my heart pounding in a way that has nothing to do with the short walk across the promenade. "I'm sorry to interrupt."

Lianne looks up, and the impact of her dark eyes

meeting mine knocks the air from my lungs. For a moment, she looks as caught off guard as I feel—her expression unguarded in a way I rarely see during our professional interactions, revealing surprise and something that might be pleasure before her professional mask starts to slide back into place.

"Cameron, what are you doing here?" There's warmth in her voice despite the surprise, and I catch the slight flush on her cheeks that suggests she's not as composed as she's trying to appear.

"Business dinner across the way," I say, gesturing toward the restaurant where McNeal and Morgan are probably watching this entire interaction and drawing their own conclusions. "I saw you through the window and I couldn't resist saying hello. I hope I'm not interrupting anything important."

"We were just finishing up," Maya says, extending her hand with a knowing smile that suggests Lianne has told her at least some version of our complicated history. "You must be Cameron Judd. I'm Maya Navarro. I've heard a lot about you."

The way she emphasizes "a lot" makes me wonder exactly what Lianne has shared about our relationship, about Santa Barbara, about the kiss in her office that I haven't been able to stop thinking about for three days.

"Miss Navarro, pleasure to meet you," I say, shaking her hand. "Declan speaks very highly of you."

"Please, call me Maya," she says, then gestures to the man sitting beside her. "This is Elliot Walker, CEO of Pierce Enterprises. And you know Declan, of course."

I hadn't noticed Declan Pierce at the table until Maya

mentioned him—he must have stepped away briefly, probably a phone call or restroom break. But now I see him approaching from the restaurant's interior, sliding his phone into his pocket with the practiced ease of someone who handles business calls during personal dinners.

I extend my hand to shake Elliot's. "Cameron Judd. Nice to meet you."

"Likewise," Elliot replies with a firm handshake and direct eye contact that suggests he's sizing me up, possibly at Maya's request.

"Sorry about that, everyone—client call that couldn't wait," Declan says as he rejoins the table, settling back into his chair with an apologetic smile. "Cameron, good to see you. How are things?"

"Very well, thanks. We should have some major partnerships locked in within the next few weeks, actually." I'm aware that I'm making small talk, that I'm prolonging this interaction beyond what's strictly necessary, but I can't seem to make myself leave when Lianne is sitting right here.

"Would you like to join us?" Lianne asks, and for a moment—one dangerous, tempting moment—I consider accepting. Consider sitting down with her and Maya and Declan and Elliot and forgetting about McNeal and Morgan entirely, letting the renewable energy deal collapse because I'd rather spend the evening watching Lianne laugh and listening to her talk about anything other than Sterling Industries' anniversary celebration.

"I wish I could, but I really should get back to my meeting," I say, though every instinct tells me to stay. "They're probably wondering if I've abandoned them entirely."

"Of course," Lianne says, and I catch a flash of something

in her expression—disappointment, maybe, or relief, or possibly both.

After saying goodbye, I return to our restaurant where Morgan and McNeal have the good grace to pretend they weren't watching my entire interaction across the promenade.

"Sorry about that," I say as I rejoin them, settling back into my chair with what I hope is professional composure. "Client coordination issue that needed immediate attention."

"No problem at all," Morgan says diplomatically. "These things happen in business. Client relationships require maintenance. Now, about the projected timeline for the Arizona facility..."

I engage with their discussion, making appropriate responses about development schedules and regulatory requirements and financial projections. I ask intelligent questions. I demonstrate that I've read their materials and understand the complexities involved.

But part of my attention—too much of my attention—remains focused on the patio across the promenade. I catch glimpses of Lianne and her companions through the evening foot traffic, watching the easy way she interacts with her friends, the genuine laughter that has nothing to do with professional courtesy or client management.

Ten minutes later, they stand from their table, gathering purses and phones in the universal signal that dinner is ending. Maya and Declan head toward the valet stand while Lianne and Elliot linger for a moment, probably exchanging final pleasantries before going their separate ways.

"Gentlemen," I say, interrupting Morgan's detailed

analysis of federal tax incentive structures with the kind of abruptness that would be rude in any other context. "I apologize, but I need to take care of something. Could we continue this discussion early next week? Say Tuesday morning?"

Both men look genuinely surprised by the abrupt conclusion to our dinner—we haven't even ordered dessert, and there were at least three more topics on McNeal's agenda—but they're too professional to question a board chair's decision to end a business meeting.

"Of course," McNeal says, already gathering his documents with the efficiency of someone who's had meetings canceled on short notice before. "We'll have our attorneys review the partnership frameworks over the weekend and get back to you with preliminary agreements by Monday."

"Perfect. Thank you both for a productive evening. I'll have my office coordinate schedules for next week." I signal for the check, settling our bill with the efficiency of someone who's conducted countless business dinners and knows exactly how to end one gracefully.

I step out onto the promenade, the evening air warm against my skin, carrying the scent of Italian food and expensive wine and the jasmine that grows in planters along the walkway.

Lianne emerges from the restaurant just then, alone now. She's moving toward what looks like a small boutique gallery at the end of the walkway, probably browsing the art in the window displays while she waits. It's such a Lianne thing to do—finding beauty and interest in unexpected places, never wasting a moment just standing around.

I approach her as she pauses in front of a gallery window,

studying an abstract painting displayed in the storefront with the kind of focused attention she brings to everything, as if the painting holds secrets that only careful observation can reveal.

"Interesting piece," I say, stopping beside her to look at the abstract painting that's caught her attention—bold splashes of red and gold against a dark background, passionate and chaotic and somehow beautiful.

She turns, and seeing her face this close, without the barrier of restaurant tables or business associates or professional pretense, sends heat racing through my bloodstream.

"Cameron." My name sounds different when she says it like this, intimate and familiar rather than professional.

"Where's everyone?"

She cocks her head toward the valet stand at the far end of the promenade. "They left first. Maya and Declan had to get back for something, and Elliot had another appointment."

"And you're..."

"Waiting for my car. Thought I'd look at some art while the valet sorts things out." She turns back to the gallery window, but I can see her reflection watching me, studying my face in the glass. "What about you? Business dinner over?"

"Just finished. Though I have to admit, I spent most of it thinking about Tuesday night."

Her reflection goes completely still, every muscle tensing at the reference to that kiss in her office. "Cameron."

"I know we agreed to keep things professional," I say, moving closer, close enough that I can smell her perfume—

something with jasmine and citrus that I've never been able to forget. "But I can't stop thinking about you."

She turns to face me fully, and there's heat in her eyes that wasn't there before we kissed, before we acknowledged that whatever this is between us isn't going away. "We're in public."

"I know. Which is why I've been going crazy since that night, having to pretend nothing's changed." I drop my voice to barely above a whisper. "But everything's changed, hasn't it? I can't keep pretending that what I feel for you is purely professional."

"We're in public," she whispers though she doesn't move away.

"Have coffee with me tomorrow," I say. "Or dinner this weekend. Let me take you somewhere we can have this conversation properly."

"What about tonight?" she asks, her voice lowering. "My place."

I frown. "Are you sure?"

"No. But the offer's there if you're interested." She pulls out her phone with slightly shaking hands. "I'll text you the address in case we get separated in traffic."

My phone buzzes a moment later with her address, and I save it immediately, as if I might forget the location between here and the valet stand.

"Don't worry," I say, meeting her eyes with a promise I intend to keep. "We won't get separated."

13

———

Lianne

My HANDS SHAKE as I unlock the door, and I'm grateful Cameron is still finding parking because it gives me a moment to breathe before he sees just how nervous I am about what I've invited him into.

Not just into my home—into my life, my heart, the carefully constructed world I've built since he walked away four years ago. This is my sanctuary, the place I retreat to when the professional mask gets too heavy, when I need to remember who I am beneath all the polish and competence.

The townhouse smells like the jasmine candles I lit last night while decompressing after a long day, before I knew I'd run into him tonight. The living room windows frame the Pacific, dark now except for the scattered lights of boats in the distance and the distant glow of the Santa Monica pier.

Everything here tells the story I wanted to tell. The cream leather sofa I saved for months to afford, working double shifts at Morrison Events to make the down payment. The Filipino art pieces that honor where I came from—a painting of a sari-sari store that reminds me of my grand-mother's neighborhood, a sculpture made from reclaimed materials that speaks to resilience and reinvention. The orchids I replace every week because I like having something alive and beautiful in my space, something that requires care and attention.

It's the home of someone who built her own success, who doesn't need anyone else's validation. But it's also lonely. Carefully arranged, perfectly controlled, designed for a woman who doesn't let anyone close enough to mess up the pristine surfaces or leave their coffee mug on the marble countertop or make the space feel lived-in rather than displayed.

This place is beautiful, but it's also safe. A fortress I built to prove I didn't need anyone.

Until tonight.

Tonight, I'm about to let someone past all those carefully constructed walls, into the space that represents everything I've accomplished without him.

The doorbell rings, and I take one last look around my perfect, controlled space before I open the door and let chaos back into my life.

Cameron is standing on my doorstep with his hands in his pockets, looking as nervous as I feel. He's loosened his tie and undone the top button of his shirt, small concessions to casualness that somehow make him more attractive rather than less polished. There's something vulnerable about seeing him like this—not the board chair or the billionaire investor, but just Cameron, standing at my door and waiting to see if I'll let him in.

"Hi," he says in a low voice that makes my pulse skip.

"Hi yourself." I step back to let him enter, hyperaware of how his presence immediately changes the energy of my space. The apartment that felt too big and too empty suddenly feels smaller, more intimate, charged with possibility.

"Can I get you something to drink? Wine? Coffee? Water?" I'm babbling, falling back on hostess mode because I don't know what else to do with my hands, with the nervous energy crackling through me.

"Wine sounds good," he says, but he's not looking at the kitchen or the wine fridge. He's taking in the details of my space, his gaze lingering on the carefully chosen art pieces, the orchids on the side table, the way the city lights reflect off the ocean in the distance. "This is beautiful, Lianne. The view is spectacular."

"I fell in love with it the moment I saw it," I admit, pulling a bottle of Sauvignon Blanc from my wine refrigerator—the same varietal we tasted in Santa Barbara, though I don't mention that. "It was completely impractical—more expensive than anything I should have been considering at the time. But I wanted to wake up every morning looking at the ocean, wanted that reminder that I'd made it far enough to afford views that people dream about."

"Smart investment," Cameron says, moving to stand by the windows, looking out at the water. "There's something about the ocean that puts everything else in perspective. Makes the daily struggles feel smaller somehow."

I pour wine into two glasses, grateful for the familiar ritual of being a hostess. It gives my hands something to do while my mind processes that Cameron Phillip Arthur Judd is standing in my living room, about to drink wine on my sofa, looking at me like I'm the most important thing in his world.

"To successful negotiations," I say as I hand him a glass, then immediately regret the reference to business when that's clearly not what we're here for.

"To second chances," Cameron counters, touching his glass to mine with a soft clink that seems to echo in the quiet apartment. "To having the courage to try again."

We settle on my sofa, close enough that I can smell his cologne—something woody and expensive that I've never been able to forget—but far enough apart that we're not quite touching. The wine helps settle my nerves, but it doesn't do anything about the electricity crackling between us or the way Cameron's eyes keep finding mine across the rim of his glass.

"This is a great neighborhood," he says, and we spend a few minutes talking about the restaurants within walking distance, the farmer's market on Sundays, the yoga studio I pretend I'll start attending someday. Safe topics that have nothing to do with why he's really here.

Then he sets down his wine glass and turns to face me more fully.

"I have a confession," he says, his voice taking on a more serious tone.

"What's that?"

"I've been thinking about this moment since Tuesday night. About being alone with you, really alone, without cleaning crews or business associates or professional obligations standing between us." He pauses, his voice dropping lower. "About what we've been missing."

My breath catches. "Cameron..."

"I can't stop thinking about that night in Santa Barbara. The way it felt to hold you again, to fall asleep with you in my arms." His eyes search mine, intense and vulnerable. "Tell me you've been thinking about it too."

I set down my wine glass, my hands trembling slightly. "Every night," I admit quietly, the truth slipping out before I can second-guess it. "I've been thinking about it every night since we left that hotel room."

Cameron sets down his wine glass and shifts closer, turning to face me fully. "I don't want to spend another four years wondering 'what if.' Not when I know how right it feels to be with you again. Not when I've finally admitted to myself that I never stopped wanting you."

The honesty in his voice, the way he's looking at me like he's seeing straight through every professional facade I've maintained, makes something flutter in my chest that has nothing to do with nerves and everything to do with want.

"I know this is complicated," he continues, reaching out to touch my face with the gentle reverence I remember from when we were together. "I know we have history and professional obligations and probably a dozen reasons why we should keep things simple. But I don't want simple. I want you. All of you. The brilliant event planner who creates magic for other people, the woman who volunteers at community centers because she believes in giving back, the person who remembers every detail about wine pairings and flowers and what makes celebrations meaningful."

Each word hits me like a caress, as if he's seeing me—really seeing me—in ways that go beyond the professional competence I've used as armor for four years.

"I want you too," I whisper, the admission slipping out before I can second-guess it.

"Are you sure?" he asks, his hand still cupping my face, thumb brushing across my cheekbone. "Because this time, I'm not running away in the morning. This time, I want to see where this leads us. I want to try to build something real."

Instead of answering with words, I kiss him.

It starts soft, familiar, like coming home after a long journey. But when Cameron responds immediately, his free hand coming up to tangle in my hair, the kiss deepens into something that speaks of second chances and the courage to risk everything again.

This is different from our desperate encounter in Santa Barbara or our interrupted moment in my office. This is happening in my home, in my space, with the conscious choice to let him back into my life completely—not just for one night, but for whatever comes next.

"Lianne..." he murmurs against my mouth, and my name sounds like a promise, like everything he's been trying to tell me since we found our way back to each other.

I respond by shifting closer, eliminating the careful distance we've maintained on my sofa. Cameron's hands frame my face as he kisses me with an intensity that makes me remember exactly why I fell for him in the first place— not just because he's beautiful, but because when he focuses on something, he gives it his complete attention.

Right now, that attention is focused entirely on me.

His hands move to my waist, pulling me closer until I'm on his lap, my body fitting against his like it's been designed for this exact moment. Every nerve ending is alive, aware of nothing else but his touch, his scent, the way his breathing changes as I press closer.

"I've tried so hard to convince myself I didn't miss this, miss you," I whisper against his lips, my hands exploring the muscles of his shoulders through the fabric of his shirt.

"How did that work out for you?" Cameron's voice is rough as his mouth moves to my neck, finding that sensitive spot just below my ear that makes me gasp and arch against him.

"Terribly," I gasp, the feel of his lips against my skin making me forget every logical reason why this might be a mistake.

His hands are everywhere now—tangling in my hair, skimming down my sides, pulling me impossibly closer as I lose myself in the sensation of being wanted this desperately by someone who matters this much.

He kisses me again, deeper this time, with the kind of focused intensity that makes everything else disappear except the feeling of his mouth on mine, his hands in my hair, the solid warmth of his body as I press closer. I can feel his arousal through the fabric of his trousers, evidence of how much he wants me sending heat spiraling through my core.

When I shift against him deliberately, the movement draws a low groan from his throat that sends my pulse racing even faster.

"God, I've missed this," he breathes against my neck, his hands still tangled in my hair. "I've missed you so much."

"I know," I whisper, my fingers tracing the line of his jaw, feeling the slight stubble there. "Me too."

He pulls back just enough to look at me, his thumb

brushing across my lower lip with such tenderness that it makes my chest ache. "I can't get enough of you."

"Then don't," I say, surprised by my own boldness, by how much I want this, want him. "Don't stop."

"Trust me, Lianne," he murmurs, his voice rough with want and promise. "I have no intention of stopping."

The heat in his voice, the way he's looking at me like I'm the only thing that matters in the world, makes every nerve ending in my body suddenly alert, alive with anticipation. When he shifts me back onto the couch and stands up, extending his hand to me, I don't hesitate.

I take it and let him pull me to my feet, the movement bringing us chest to chest, so close that I can feel his heart beating as fast as mine.

"Come here," he whispers, and then his mouth is on mine again, more urgent this time, more demanding as I melt into him, my hands finding the buttons of his shirt because suddenly anything standing between us is a barrier I need gone.

From there, it's a slow dance toward the stairs that lead to my bedroom, Cameron's hands everywhere—tangling in my hair, tracing the line of my spine, finding the zipper at the back of my dress with a familiar skill that reminds me he knows my body, still knows what makes me respond.

"God, you're beautiful," he murmurs against my neck as we climb the stairs. "Do you know how many nights I've thought about this? About having you in my arms again?"

"Tell me," I breathe, because I need to hear it, need to know that the longing hasn't been one-sided.

"Every night," he admits, his hands framing my face as we reach the top of the stairs and he looks at me with an intensity that makes my knees weak. "Every single night for four years, I've wondered what would have happened if I'd been brave enough to fight for us instead of letting you go."

The admission breaks something open in my chest, something I've kept carefully locked away since the day he chose his family's approval over what we had together.

But tonight isn't about the past. Tonight is about choosing to trust him with my heart again, about believing that people can change and that some love stories deserve a second chapter.

We reach my bedroom, and I guide him toward my most private space, the room where I've spent countless nights alone, building my business and my walls in equal measure. Letting him in here feels like the ultimate act of faith.

As if he can sense my hesitation, Cameron pauses just inside the doorway. "We don't have to do this if you're not ready. We can just talk, or I can go—"

"I want to," I say firmly, pulling him inside and closing the door behind us with a soft click that seems to reverberate through my entire body. "I want this. I want you."

His mouth finds mine again, and this time there's nothing tentative about his touch. He guides me toward the bed, and I let him, my body fitting against his like it was designed for this moment, for this man.

When the dress is gone, leaving me in nothing but my underwear, Cameron leans back to take me in, his gaze following the line of my body from head to toe with such reverence that it makes me feel beautiful, desired, seen.

"You're so beautiful," he murmurs, his fingers tracing the curve of my collarbone, down to my breast. "Every part of you is perfect."

His words send heat spiraling through me, making me feel wanted in ways I've forgotten existed. I pull him back to me, needing his weight on top of me, his mouth against mine, the reassurance that he's really here, that this is real and not just another dream I'll wake up from alone.

My hands find the buttons of his shirt, tugging it off with an urgency that comes from knowing we've waited too long to hold back now. Skin against skin, his mouth finding my neck, my collarbone, my breasts, his hands sliding up my thighs until he can slip my underwear off, leaving me completely naked beneath him.

"I want to taste you," he murmurs against my hip, his tongue tracing the curve of my waist and moving lower.

When his tongue finds me, I gasp, my fingers digging into the sheets as sensation builds. He knows exactly how to touch me, how to bring me to the edge and hold me there until I'm begging for release.

The orgasm crashes over me in waves, my body pulsing as he holds me in place with one strong hand, his mouth working me through every aftershock until I'm boneless and breathless.

When I come back to myself, he moves up the bed, his mouth finding mine again. I can taste myself on him, and it makes me shiver with renewed desire.

He reaches for his pants, retrieving a condom and sliding it on with hands that shake slightly—the only sign that he's as affected by this as I am.

I feel him press against my entrance, the blunt head of his cock a promise of what's to come.

"Please," I whisper, and he pushes inside me slowly, filling me inch by inch until I'm completely full.

"God, you feel so good," he says, his forehead pressed against mine, his breathing ragged.

"So do you," I manage, trying to ignore the emotional impact of having him inside me again, of feeling so connected to someone I thought I'd never let myself trust again.

He starts to move, slow and deep strokes that make me moan and arch against him. It feels so right, like every part of me has been waiting for this moment, for him.

When he flips me on top, his hands gripping my hips as I ride him, my fingers digging into his shoulders for leverage, I feel powerful and vulnerable all at once.

"Let go, baby," he urges, his voice rough. "Let go for me."

The orgasm rolls through me like a wave, breaking over me with a force that makes me cry out his name.

He follows soon after, my name on his lips as he buries his face in my neck, his body shuddering against mine.

We lie there afterward, both of us struggling to catch our breath, overwhelmed by the intimacy of what just happened.

"I've never stopped thinking about you, Lianne," he says, his voice thick with emotion. "I don't think I ever will."

I turn to look at him—really look at him—at the way his hair is messy from my fingers, at the way his eyes are soft and vulnerable, at the way his hands are still skimming up and down my sides like he can't stop touching me.

"I've missed you too," I admit. "I've missed us."

"Can we make this work?" he asks quietly. "Can we find a way to make this work when we've both hurt each other so much?"

The question is valid, but I'm not ready to answer it yet.

Not when I'm still processing what just happened, what it means that I let him back in.

"Stay with me tonight," I whisper instead, resting my head against his shoulder.

"Wild horses couldn't drag me away," he promises, pressing a soft kiss to my temple.

After a quick trip to the bathroom, he returns to bed and pulls me close. I rest my head against his chest, the steady beat of his heart lulling me toward sleep.

And for the first time in a long time, I let myself dream of a future that includes him.

A future that goes beyond business and professional success to something real and meaningful and lasting.

A future that might actually be worth the risk.

14

———

Cameron

I WAKE before dawn to the sound of waves and the feeling of Lianne's body curved perfectly against mine.

For a moment, I lie still in the gray pre-dawn light, afraid that moving might break the spell. Her head is on my chest, dark hair spilled across my shoulder, one hand resting over my heart like she's claiming it even in sleep.

This is what I threw away four years ago. This feeling of absolute rightness, of being exactly where I belong.

But it's different now. Stronger. Four years ago, what we had was intense and passionate and real, but it was also fragile. We were both trying to figure out who we were while navigating complications of different worlds.

Now we've both done the work of becoming ourselves. We can choose each other from a place of strength rather than need.

The woman in my arms isn't the junior event planner I fell in love with during Sophia's wedding. She's built an empire through determination, commands boardrooms, creates magic for others. She's more confident, more herself in ways that take my breath away.

And somehow, she's chosen to trust me again.

Lianne stirs against me, a soft sound that's half-sigh, half-contentment. When she tilts her head back to look at me, her dark eyes are soft with sleep but completely aware.

"Good morning," she says, her husky voice sending heat through me.

"Good morning, beautiful." I brush hair away from her face, marveling at how she leans into the touch without hesitation. "Sleep well?"

"Better than I have in weeks," she admits. "You?"

"Perfect. Absolutely perfect."

She smiles, and I'm struck again by how different this feels from Santa Barbara. Back then, there was desperation, urgency of rediscovering each other. This morning, it feels like we're building something that can last.

"What time is it?" she asks.

I glance at the clock. "Just after six."

She shifts against me, the movement bringing her body into perfect alignment with mine, reminding us both that we're naked under these sheets.

"Do you have somewhere you need to be?"

"Nowhere more important than right here."

Lianne props herself up on one elbow, the sheet slipping to reveal the elegant line of her shoulder. "I don't think I've ever seen you this relaxed. Even back then, you were always thinking about the next meeting, the next obligation."

She's not wrong. Even when we were together, part of my mind was always occupied with business or family expectations or keeping our relationship secret.

"Maybe I've learned what's actually important," I say, catching her hand and pressing a kiss to her palm.

"And what's that?"

"This. You. Us. The way you look at me like I'm someone worth trusting again."

Lianne's hands come up to frame my face, thumbs brushing across my cheekbones with infinite tenderness. "You are worth trusting. I wouldn't be here if I didn't believe that."

The confession breaks something open in my chest. When I kiss her, it's with the desperate gratitude of someone given a second chance at something precious.

We make love again, slower this time, more deliberate. A claiming that goes both ways. When we're both spent and tangled together, Lianne traces patterns on my chest with one finger.

"I should probably get up," she says eventually, though she makes no move to leave my arms. "Make coffee, start the day like a responsible adult."

"Responsibility is overrated," I reply, tightening my hold on her.

She laughs, bright and unguarded. "Is that so? And what exactly constitutes irresponsible behavior?"

"Staying in bed until noon. Pretending the rest of the world doesn't exist."

"Tempting. But I actually do make excellent coffee, and I'm suddenly starving."

"Fair enough. But I'm helping with breakfast."

She pulls back with raised eyebrows. "You cook?"

"I've learned a few things in four years. Nothing fancy, but I can manage eggs without burning down your kitchen."

"Now that I have to see."

As we reluctantly disentangle, I catch sight of my phone on her nightstand and make a conscious choice. I pick it up and power it off completely.

Lianne notices. "No interruptions?"

"Not today. The world can survive without me for a few hours."

Something shifts in her expression—relief, maybe hope. "Are you sure? What if it's important?"

"Nothing is more important than this. Than us. I learned that lesson the hard way."

Twenty minutes later, we're in her kitchen, working together with easy domesticity that feels both foreign and perfectly natural.

"French press or espresso machine?" she asks.

"Whatever you prefer. I'm not picky about caffeine delivery."

She starts coffee while I handle eggs, and we fall into an easy rhythm. It's such a simple thing, but it feels significant —like we're practicing for a future that includes shared mornings.

"So," Lianne says as she arranges fresh fruit with the same attention she brings to her events, "what do you think this means? Last night, this morning... us?"

It's a fair question. Four years ago, we never really defined what we were, never talked about what we wanted. That uncertainty made us vulnerable to outside pressure.

"I think it means I want to try again," I say. "I want to

build something real this time, something that can withstand whatever complications come."

Lianne sets down the fruit plate and turns to face me, expression serious and hopeful. "And your family? Your business obligations? All the things that came between us before?" Her voice drops to a whisper. "What's different this time?"

The vulnerability in her voice breaks my heart. This is what I did to us—created doubt that lingers even now.

"What's different is that I'm not the same man who let other people make decisions about my life," I say, moving closer to frame her face with my hands. "I'm not twenty-six anymore, Lianne. I'm not going to let anyone else choose who I spend my life with."

"But they'll try. Your parents, your social circle—they'll find ways to pressure you like before."

"Let them try. I've spent four years building Sterling Industries independently, proving I don't need their approval or their money to succeed. The only approval that matters to me now is yours."

Lianne searches my face, looking for any sign of the uncertainty that destroyed us. Whatever she sees must satisfy her, because her expression softens into hope mixed with relief.

"I avoided being alone with you after Santa Barbara because I was terrified of believing in us again," she admits. "I was scared that if I let myself hope, you'd choose them over me like you did before."

"Never again," I promise, leaning down to brush my lips against hers. "You're not just some unfinished business to me. What we have now... it's real. It matters."

"It matters to me too," she whispers. "More than I thought possible."

Later, as we're finishing breakfast, I remember something I've been meaning to ask.

"My niece Lily's birthday party is next Saturday," I say, trying to keep my tone casual. "She's turning seven. There'll be a bouncy castle, face painting, the works. I'd love it if you'd come with me."

Lianne's expression shifts, something guarded sliding into place. "Cameron..."

"I know it's family, but it's just a kids' party. Low-key, not some formal—"

"I can't," she interrupts gently, setting down her coffee cup. "I'm your event planner for the gala. If we're seen together publicly before then, it could create... complications. People talk, especially in your circles."

She's right, and I know it. People would definitely talk.

"The gala is in two weeks," Lianne adds, reaching across the table for my hand. "After that, we can figure out how to navigate everything else. But right now, I need to maintain professional boundaries. For both our sakes."

I turn her hand over in mine, tracing the lines of her palm. "I don't like it."

"I don't either. But I've worked too hard to build Luminous Events to have people question my professionalism or suggest I got the Sterling contract because of personal connections."

"No one would think that. Your work speaks for itself."

"You know that's not how the world works." Her voice is

gentle but firm. "Especially not for someone like me. I'll always have to work twice as hard to prove I earned my place."

The reminder of the obstacles she faces—obstacles that don't exist for people born into families like mine—makes me want to fight harder. But I also know she's right about protecting her professional reputation.

"Okay," I concede. "But after the gala, I'm not hiding anything. I want to be able to take you to dinner, to events, to introduce you as my girlfriend without worrying about what anyone thinks."

"Girlfriend?" She raises an eyebrow, a small smile playing at her lips.

"Is that okay? Or do you prefer something else? Partner? Significant other? The woman I'm completely gone for?"

Lianne laughs, the sound warm and genuine. "Girlfriend works. Though I do like 'the woman you're completely gone for.'"

"Then that's what you are." I bring her hand to my lips, pressing a kiss to her knuckles. "Even if I can't take you to seven-year-old birthday parties for the next two weeks."

"I'm sorry," she says softly. "I know it's not ideal."

"It's okay. I understand. And you're right—we need to protect what you've built." I pause, meeting her eyes. "But Lianne? After the gala, no more hiding. Deal?"

"Deal," she agrees.

But even as she says it, I catch a flicker of something in her expression—worry, maybe, or uncertainty. As if she's already imagining the complications that will come when my family finds out about us.

I want to promise her it'll be fine, that my parents will come around, that love will be enough this time.

But the truth is, I don't know what will happen when I tell them about us. I just know that this time, I'm not letting them take her away from me.

This time, I'm choosing her.

No matter what it costs.

Lianne

"The Martinez reception needs to accommodate the bride's gluten-free requirements," Amanda says, consulting her tablet. "Should we do a separate dessert station or integrate options into the main display?"

"Separate station," I say absently, my attention split between the weekly team meeting and the iPad balanced on my lap, the screen displaying three weeks of calendar entries.

Around me, everyone is abuzz with familiar energy—Terry spreading fabric swatches across the table in rainbows of silk and satin, Sandra consulting vendor timelines with the intensity of someone managing a military operation, Amanda taking careful notes about every decision.

But while my team discusses table linens and appetizer presentations for the Martinez wedding, I'm scrolling through calendar entries that started the morning after Cameron spent the night at my townhouse. Each entry reading like evidence of how completely my professional boundaries have collapsed, how thoroughly I've let personal feelings compromise my carefully constructed career.

Tuesday, March 15, 7:00 AM — Coffee with C before vendor meeting

I remember that morning with painful clarity. Cameron appearing at my office with two cups from the café down the street, somehow knowing without asking that I'd be stressed about presentations. The way he'd set my cup down exactly where I like it—right side of my desk, within easy reach but not so close I'd knock it over while gesturing during calls.

The way his hands had found the knots between my shoulder blades while I reviewed contracts, his touch both comforting and electrifying, professional massage blurring into something more intimate as his fingers worked out tension I'd been carrying for days.

"You don't have to be perfect at everything," he'd murmured against my ear, his breath warm on my neck.

"Says the man whose company expects nothing less than perfection in every detail."

"I'm not talking about Sterling or event planning. I'm talking about us. About letting yourself be human instead of performing competence every moment."

Us. Three weeks ago, it felt like a declaration. Now it feels naive, like evidence of how easily I let hope override experience.

"Lianne?" Amanda's voice pulls me back to the present. "The ceremony timeline? For the Martinez wedding?"

"Right. Starts at four, cocktail hour immediately following." I force myself to focus, to be present for my team even though my mind is spinning. "No gaps in service. Continuous flow from ceremony through reception."

Saturday, March 19, 9:00 AM — Farmers' market

The Santa Monica Farmers' Market had become our weekend ritual with surprising speed. Cameron carrying my canvas bags, learning vendor names, developing opinions about heirloom tomatoes versus standard varieties. His genuine interest in Mrs. Chavez's strawberry cultivation methods, his willingness to taste samples of artisan honey while discussing subtle flavor differences.

Mrs. Chavez at the strawberry stand had beamed at us that first Saturday. "You two are here together! Such a lovely couple. Will I see you next week?"

Cameron had kissed me right there between the tomato display and the honey vendor, his lips sweet with berry juice, his arm solid around my waist. "You'll definitely see us next week. And the week after that."

"I've never been happier about losing my independence to farmers' market routines," he'd admitted while we walked back to my car, our bags full of produce we'd use to cook together later.

The memory makes my chest tight with something between longing and regret. Three weeks of falling back into each other, of building routines that felt permanent, of letting myself believe that maybe this time would be different.

I flip to last weekend's entries, my stomach churning.

Saturday, March 26 — Malibu site visit (work) Sunday, March 27 — Brunch with Maya

But something about the pattern bothers me as I scroll through weeks of careful documentation. All our time together happens in my space, my world, on my terms. Dinners at restaurants I choose. Mornings at the farmers' market near my townhouse. Evenings cooking in my kitchen while music plays from my speakers.

That's because I can't be seen in his world. Not while Luminous Events is planning his gala event. And while it stings—I've never been to his place in Malibu, never around his friends or social circles, never integrated into his actual life beyond the carefully contained bubble we've created—we don't have a choice.

At least, that's what I tell myself.

After all, I'm the one breaking the non-fraternization clause in the contracts we've signed when Cameron chose Luminous Events to take over planning of Sterling's gala. I'm the one harboring all the guilt over this whole... affair.

Out of habit, needing distraction from uncomfortable thoughts, I open Instagram to check industry accounts. The first few posts are standard luxury event content. A Malibu wedding with cascading orchids and sunset ceremony. A corporate gala at the Beverly Hills Hotel with ice sculptures and champagne towers. A charity auction in Newport Beach with celebrity guests and designer gowns.

Then I see it, and my heart stops.

Not a sponsored post or professional content. Just a casual share from an Instagram account I follow because they sometimes feature events I've planned. But this time it's not my work—it's someone else's party, tagged with location and date stamp that makes my stomach drop.

#BelAirBirthday   #LuxuryKidsParty   #AlessandraJudd-Martinelli

A carousel of photos from an elaborate children's birthday celebration that looks like it cost more than most weddings. Professional photography captures full carnival setup—actual carousel with hand-painted horses, cotton candy machines styled in pink and gold, what appears to be an actual ferris wheel installed in a Bel Air backyard that probably required permits and structural engineering.

But it's the third slide that steals my breath and makes the room tilt sideways.

Cameron, devastatingly handsome in a navy blazer that emphasizes his broad shoulders, standing next to the most beautiful woman I've ever seen in person or photograph. Blonde hair falling in perfect waves, champagne-colored dress that probably costs more than my monthly mortgage, her hand resting casually on his arm with the familiarity of someone completely comfortable in his space.

The caption reads: *Gorgeous celebration for little Alessandra Judd-Martinelli's 3rd birthday! Uncle Cameron looked so handsome with family friend Isabella Vitale. These two are giving us serious power couple vibes!* 😊 *#PowerCouple #Goals*

Alessandra Judd-Martinelli. The name registers slowly through my shock. Cameron's niece. Sophia's daughter. The three-year-old whose birthday party was last weekend—the same weekend he'd asked me to go with him but I told him I couldn't, not while I was planning the gala.

Now I'm staring at photos of Cameron with Isabella Vitale at the exact event I declined, where she clearly fit in effortlessly while I was across town discussing floral arrangements and menu modifications.

My hands shake as I scroll through comments, each one feeling like a knife twisting deeper:

"They look AMAZING together! When's the wedding??"

"Isabella is so gorgeous and from such a good family. Perfect match!"

"Finally! Cameron needs someone who understands his world."

"Someone from his own circle" appears multiple times in various forms, the phrase echoing with implications I can't ignore.

Someone from his own circle. Someone who belongs in his world without explanation or accommodation. Someone who can attend his niece's birthday party without it being a whole complicated thing requiring preparation and anxiety.

Suddenly I'm twelve years old again, standing in my third foster home's hallway while Mrs. Patterson explains to her sister on the phone why I'd have to be moved to another placement.

"She's a sweet girl, really she is. But she's just not quite the right fit for our family. The other children... well, you understand. Sometimes these placements just don't work out the way we hope."

Not quite the right fit. The story of my entire childhood —I was temporary, replaceable, never quite enough to be chosen permanently. Never quite fitting into families that looked perfect on paper but never felt like home because I was always the outsider, always the one who didn't quite belong.

"Lianne?" Terry's voice cuts through my spiral, concern evident in her tone. "Are you okay?"

I quickly close Instagram, but my hands are shaking so badly I nearly drop my iPad. "Just tired. Final week stress catching up with me."

"Maybe you should eat something," Sandra suggests gently, exchanging worried glances with Amanda. "You've been running on coffee and adrenaline for weeks."

"I'm fine. Really." I force brightness into my voice, trying to recover professional composure. "Let's finish the Martinez timeline."

But I'm not fine. I'm spiraling, falling back into old patterns of fear and insecurity I thought I'd outgrown through years of therapy and hard-won success.

Because despite everything I've accomplished—the business I've built, the reputation I've earned, the financial security I've created—I'm still that foster kid terrified of not being chosen, of not belonging, of being temporary in everyone's life because that's what I've always been.

After my team files out, concerned glances lingering despite my protests, I'm alone with my shattered illusions and that Instagram post burning in my memory like evidence of everything I feared.

I could call him. Ask about Isabella, about why he didn't mention the party in more detail, about what "family friend" actually means when someone's hand rests that comfortably on your arm.

But that would mean admitting I've been stalking his social media like some insecure girlfriend instead of the confident professional I've worked so hard to become. It would mean showing him that despite everything I've accomplished, I'm still vulnerable to the same insecurities that made his family's judgment so devastating four years ago.

My phone buzzes, making me jump.

CAMERON:

Missing you. Thinking about last night.
Can't wait to see you tonight.

Last night had been perfect. We'd made love, then fallen asleep tangled together while he traced patterns on my back and whispered about futures that felt possible in the darkness. I'd felt completely secure that this was real, that he'd chosen me, that we were building something that could last.

Now I'm wondering if I'm living in a fantasy while he navigates the reality of family expectations that will always take precedence over whatever we have.

Before I can process this emotional whiplash, another notification appears—an email from Sharon Finnegan, Cameron's executive assistant. The subject line makes my stomach drop: "Sterling Gala - Final Seating Adjustments."

I open it with dread pooling in my gut.

Hi Lianne,

Everything looks spectacular for Saturday! One tiny adjustment to the seating chart—we need to add Isabella Vitale at table one, seated next to Cameron Judd. The Vitale family will be joining us as special guests, and Mr. Judd requested she be positioned there for optimal conversation during dinner.

I know it's last-minute, but I'm sure you can work your magic as always.

Looking forward to an amazing evening!

Best,

Sharon

I read it three times, each word settling like lead in my chest.

Isabella Vitale. Seated next to Cameron. At table one—the VIP table, the power table, the table where Sterling

Industries' most important guests and executives will spend the evening.

At my event, where I'll be coordinating their perfect evening while they sit together like the power couple those Instagram comments claimed they were.

This is exactly how it started four years ago—Cameron making choices about his social world without including me, then expecting me to smile and accommodate whatever his family needed. Him moving through spaces where I didn't belong, with people who fit effortlessly while I worked to prove I deserved to be there.

I swore I'd never put myself in that position again. Swore I'd never be the woman who smiled through her own heartbreak while facilitating someone else's romance.

The irony is suffocating. I'll be the one ensuring their crystal glasses stay filled, their conversation flows smoothly, their every need met with the seamless service that's made Luminous Events successful.

I'll facilitate their romance while wearing a headset and clipboard that announce exactly what I am—the help. The event planner. The person who creates magic for other people's lives while her own falls apart.

My phone rings. Cameron's name flashing with that photo of him laughing that I took last weekend at the farmers' market, both of us happy and hopeful and apparently delusional about what we were building.

The same weekend when he'd kissed me and told Mrs. Chavez we were a couple, making promises in public that felt real until I saw him with Isabella at his niece's birthday party.

For the first time in three weeks, that photo doesn't make

me smile. It makes me feel naive and foolish, like someone who believed in fairy tales despite every lesson life taught her about the temporary nature of belonging.

I let it go to voicemail, unable to hear his voice without my carefully constructed composure crumbling completely.

Almost immediately, a voicemail notification appears. Against my better judgment—against every self-protective instinct screaming at me to maintain distance—I play it.

"Hey, beautiful. Just wanted to hear your voice before my afternoon meetings. I know you're swamped with final preparations, but I can't stop thinking about last night. The way you fell asleep in my arms, how perfect you looked this morning making coffee in my shirt. I'm counting down until I see you again tonight. Call me when you get a chance."

The warmth in his voice, the casual intimacy of "beautiful" and remembering details like me wearing his shirt—it should reassure me. Should make me feel chosen and wanted.

Instead, it feels like evidence of how compartmentalized his life is. How easily he can whisper sweet words in private while his family parades suitable alternatives in front of him. How he can be intimate with me in the darkness while Isabella Vitale stands beside him in the daylight, her hand comfortable on his arm like she belongs there.

The message should warm me, should reassure me that last night meant something. Instead, it feels like evidence of how compartmentalized his life is—how easily he can be intimate with me in private while maintaining separate social obligations that don't include me.

I delete the voicemail without calling back, my hands shaking with emotions I can't name. Anger. Hurt. Fear. The bone-deep terror that I'm repeating old patterns, that I've let myself become temporary in someone's life again, that the moment real life intrudes I'll be replaced by someone more suitable.

Outside my windows, Los Angeles spreads out in afternoon sunshine that feels too bright, too cheerful for my emotional state. In forty-eight hours, this view will be filled with people celebrating Sterling's anniversary—beautiful people in expensive clothes, sipping wine I selected, enjoying an event I've spent months perfecting.

The event will be a success. Luminous Events will receive glowing reviews, new referrals, industry recognition that proves we're the real deal.

I should be thrilled. Should be celebrating the professional triumph that validates everything I've worked for.

But all I can think about is that scared little girl who learned early that no matter how good you are, how hard you try, how much you accomplish, there's always someone more suitable waiting to take your place.

And sometimes, the people you love most are the ones who do the replacing.

My phone buzzes again. Another text from Cameron.

CAMERON:

Everything okay? You usually respond
faster. Getting worried.

I stare at the message, at evidence that he notices my patterns, that he pays attention to details like response times and emotional shifts.

But he didn't notice—or didn't think to mention—that bringing Isabella to his niece's birthday party while building a relationship with me might send mixed messages. Didn't think about how requesting she sit next to him at the gala I'm planning might feel like a betrayal.

Or maybe he did notice, and this is exactly what he wants—me in the background creating magic while he builds his actual life with someone appropriate.

I don't respond. Can't figure out what to say that won't reveal how completely I'm falling apart, how thoroughly that Instagram post destroyed the fragile hope I'd been building.

Instead, I pull out my event coordination binder and start reviewing final details for Saturday night. Seating charts that now include Isabella Vitale at table one. Timeline specifications for an evening that will probably break my heart. Vendor confirmations for services that will ensure Cameron and Isabella have a perfect night.

This is what I do. I create magic for other people, make their moments perfect, ensure their celebrations exceed expectations.

I just forgot—again—that I was never supposed to believe in the magic myself.

That some roles are temporary by design, that some people are meant to facilitate rather than participate, that sometimes love isn't enough when the whole world is designed to remind you that you don't quite fit.

Saturday night will be perfect. Professional. Flawless.

And it will probably destroy me.

But I'll smile through it with the same grace I've shown through every other impossible situation, because that's what survivors do—we adapt, we endure, we smile through pain that no one else sees.

We survive.

16

Lianne

Isabella Vitale.

The elegant script mocks me as I set the cream card stock next to Cameron's nameplate at Table One.

I've known this was coming since Sharon's email. Ever since I saw those Instagram photos and realized what I was really coordinating—not just Sterling Industries' anniversary, but the perfect romantic evening for Cameron to celebrate with someone who actually belongs in his world.

The first guests are arriving at the Esperanza Resort. No more torturing myself with what-ifs.

It's here. The moment I've been dreading since I placed that seating card next to Cameron's name, since I understood what tonight really means.

It had always been a job, wasn't it? The biggest event my company has ever organized, one I can't mess up.

Not even if it ends up breaking my heart all over again.

"Lianne!" Amanda appears at my elbow, headset on, iPad in hand, her energy focused and professional. "The photography team needs approval for the red-carpet setup, and catering wants confirmation on wine service timing."

I nod, forcing myself to step away from Table One before I do something unprofessional like sweep Isabella's place card onto the floor and pretend it never existed. "Handle the photographers. I'll check with catering personally."

The Grand Ballroom buzzes with controlled chaos that would overwhelm anyone unfamiliar with high-stakes event coordination. Servers in crisp white uniforms adjust already perfect place settings with the precision of people who know they're being watched. Florists add final touches to center-pieces of white peonies—*peonies*, because Cameron remembered they were my favorite—and gold accents that catch the evening light. Musicians tune instruments, the discordant sounds gradually resolving into harmony.

Everything is proceeding exactly according to plan. This will be the kind of celebration that generates magazine features and referral business for years, that establishes Luminous Events as the premier luxury planner in Los Angeles.

But all I can think about is the woman who'll be sitting next to Cameron in two hours, her hand comfortable on his arm like it belongs there.

Through floor-to-ceiling windows, I can see luxury cars arriving at the circular drive—Bentleys and Rolls-Royces and Tesla Models that cost more than most houses. Board members from New York and London, tech industry leaders whose companies shape the future, families whose names appear on museum wings and hospital buildings. Cameron's people, gathering to celebrate fifty years of success that builds legacies and shapes dynasties.

My earpiece crackles with updates from my team scattered throughout the venue. "VIP guests arriving at main entrance." "Media setup complete on terrace." "Orchestra ready for seven o'clock start."

Every detail coordinated, every contingency planned for, every element designed to create an unforgettable evening that will be discussed in industry circles for months.

I'm coordinating with the sommelier about wine service timing when I catch sight of familiar broad shoulders near the ballroom entrance. Cameron, devastating in a perfectly tailored tuxedo that emphasizes his lean strength, greeting early arrivals with the confident charm of someone completely comfortable in his role as host.

He's in full board chair mode, working the room with effortless grace that comes from a lifetime of training. This is Cameron in his natural element—wealthy, powerful, completely at home in a world of inherited privilege and strategic networking.

A world where I'll always be the hired help, no matter how successful my business becomes. No matter how many events I coordinate or how glowing my reviews are.

"Lianne." His voice behind me makes me startle, pulling me from coordination mode into personal awareness I can't afford right now. "We need to talk."

I fall back on my only armor—professional distance that's kept me functional for the past week. "Is there something about the event that requires adjustment? Last-minute changes to the timeline?"

"You know damn well this isn't about the event." Cameron steps closer, lowering his voice so nearby servers won't overhear. "You've been avoiding me for days. Routing everything through Amanda, dodging my calls. What the hell is going on?"

Before I can respond—before I can figure out what to say that won't reveal how completely I'm falling apart—my earpiece crackles with urgent communication from Amanda. "We have a situation with the floral arrangements on Table Twelve."

I press my earpiece, grateful for the interruption. "On my way."

"Lianne—" Cameron starts, frustration evident in his voice.

But I'm already moving, using vendor crises as a shield against conversations I'm not ready to have.

The floral issue takes ten minutes—a simple adjustment that could have waited, honestly, but I milk it for every second of distance it provides. When I return to the main ballroom, Cameron is surrounded by board members from the New York office, deep in business conversation about quarterly projections and market positioning.

Back in his element. The kind of sophisticated financial discourse I'll never be equipped to join, where people discuss millions like I discuss hundreds, where casual references to vacation homes and private schools assume a shared understanding of privilege I'll never possess.

"Lianne, the Judd family just arrived!" Amanda's voice carries excitement through my earpiece, and I force myself to look toward the entrance.

I watch Mrs. Judd make her entrance in elegant midnight-blue silk that probably cost more than my first car, her posture impeccable, her smile gracious and practiced. Mr. Judd carries himself with the bearing that draws every eye—the confidence of someone who's never questioned whether he belongs anywhere.

And between them, looking like she stepped out of a European fashion magazine, is Isabella Vitale.

The Instagram photos didn't do her justice. Not even close.

She's even more beautiful in person, with an ethereal quality that makes everyone else seem slightly out of focus. Blond hair catching light from crystal chandeliers like spun gold, champagne-colored gown flowing like liquid silk with every movement. But it's not just physical beauty—it's the way she carries herself. Confident without arrogance. Gracious without seeming rehearsed. Like she's never questioned her place in rooms like this because she was born to grace them, was raised from childhood to navigate these spaces with ease.

This is the woman Cameron's parents want for him. This is the woman who belongs at Table One while I coordinate from the sidelines, my headset and clipboard announcing exactly what I am.

Through the crowd, I catch glimpses of Cameron approaching his family. I can see the moment he spots Isabella—his posture straightens slightly, a genuine smile spreading across his face, the ease with which he greets her suggesting comfort and familiarity.

They embrace warmly, her hand remaining on his arm in a gesture that speaks to years of knowing each other, of shared history and mutual understanding. Not possessive, but comfortable. Natural.

As if sensing my attention across the ballroom, Cameron's gaze finds mine. For a moment, something flickers in his eyes—confusion, maybe concern, possibly guilt.

But Isabella says something that makes him laugh, that private laugh I thought was reserved for me, and his attention returns to her completely.

The next hour passes in a blur of controlled chaos. Cocktail hour proceeds flawlessly—guests mingling on the terrace under string lights and California stars, servers circulating with the champagne and Sauvignon Blanc we selected together in Santa Barbara, orchestra providing elegant background music that sets the perfect tone.

From my position managing logistics, coordinating staff movements and timing like a conductor leading an orchestra, I watch Cameron work the room. And through it all, Isabella remains at his side.

Not clinging or demanding attention, but present in a way that suggests she belongs there. She contributes intelligently to business conversations about renewable energy and European market expansion. When elderly board members share stories about Sterling's early days, she listens with engaged attention that seems genuine rather than performative. She laughs at appropriate moments, asks thoughtful questions, enhances every interaction simply by participating.

She doesn't complicate Cameron's networking. She enhances it. This is what a suitable partner looks like in his world—someone who makes his life easier simply by being herself, who requires no accommodation or explanation.

They don't just look perfect together—they look inevitable together.

"Lianne." A cultured voice behind me makes me turn. "I

thought it was you, though I confess I didn't make the connection until just now."

Mrs. Judd stands before me in her midnight-blue silk, her expression warm but calculating in ways that make my stomach drop. She's holding a champagne flute, her posture relaxed, but there's purpose in her eyes.

I force neutral politeness despite my racing heart. "Mrs. Judd. Good evening. I trust everything is meeting your expectations?"

"The event is absolutely exquisite, dear. Truly sophisticated beyond what I anticipated." Her tone carries genuine appreciation, which somehow makes what's coming worse. "When Cameron mentioned hiring Luminous Events, I didn't realize..." She pauses meaningfully. "Well, I didn't realize you were the Lianne behind Luminous Events. The owner. How remarkable."

"Thank you," I manage. "We've worked hard to build our reputation."

"I can see that. The attention to detail is extraordinary. These peonies, for instance—" she gestures to the center-pieces, "—they're out of season, aren't they? Must have cost a fortune to source. Someone with excellent taste chose them."

The observation feels loaded, like she knows Cameron suggested them, knows they're my favorite flowers, is piecing together exactly why her son has been so mysteriously involved in the planning process.

"We always strive to exceed expectations," I reply carefully.

Mrs. Judd takes a delicate sip of champagne, her eyes never leaving my face. "You know, dear, I've been thinking about your journey. From foster care to this—building a successful event planning company in one of the most competitive markets in the country. It's quite an achievement."

The mention of foster care hits like a slap, delivered with such casual precision that I know it's intentional. She's researched me, or remembered me from four years ago, is making sure I understand she knows exactly where I came from.

"I've been fortunate," I say, my voice tight.

"Fortunate, yes. But also clearly talented and determined." She glances around the ballroom with satisfaction. "It takes remarkable resilience to build something from nothing. To succeed when you don't have family connections or financial security as a safety net. Most people in your situation wouldn't have made it this far."

Most people in your situation. The words hang between us, polite but pointed.

"I had good mentors," I reply, refusing to give her the satisfaction of seeing how her words cut.

"I'm sure you did." Mrs. Judd's smile doesn't reach her eyes. "And you've clearly learned to navigate worlds that must have seemed very foreign at first. To understand what people like us expect, what we value. That kind of adaptability is admirable."

People like us.

People unlike me. The distinction couldn't be clearer.

"Though I have to say," she continues, her voice dropping slightly, conspiratorially, "I'm beginning to understand why Cameron has been so unusually involved in this planning process. His insistence on approving every detail, his personal attendance at vendor meetings. It seemed excessive for a board chair with global responsibilities, but now…"

"Mr. Judd takes Sterling's reputation very seriously," I say, my heart pounding. "This anniversary is important to the company's positioning."

"Oh, I'm sure that's part of it." Mrs. Judd's tone suggests she doesn't believe a word. "But you and I both know my son well enough to recognize when there's more to a story than professional diligence."

She pauses, studying my face with uncomfortable intensity. "You know, it's interesting. Four years ago, Cameron dated an event planner. A lovely girl, but ultimately not quite right for our family. Different backgrounds, different values. It ended badly, as these things often do when people from incompatible worlds try to force something that simply doesn't fit."

The casual cruelty of it—reducing our entire relationship to "not quite right," suggesting our breakup was inevitable rather than the result of her family's pressure—makes my throat tight.

"I'm sure every family has their own criteria," I manage.

"Indeed. And ours are quite specific, as I'm sure you can understand." Mrs. Judd glances toward where Cameron and Isabella are engaged in animated conversation. "It's so wonderful to see Cameron connecting with someone who truly understands his world. Someone who can be a real partner in all aspects of his life—social, professional, personal. Someone whose family understands the responsibilities that come with wealth and position."

Someone whose family. Not someone who came from

nowhere, who built something from nothing, who has no family history to leverage or legacy to honor.

"Isabella is remarkable," Mrs. Judd continues, her voice warm with approval. "Accomplished, well-educated, from a family that understands international business and social obligation. She knows what's expected of someone in Cameron's position, what demands will be placed on his partner. That kind of understanding is invaluable."

The implication is crystal clear—Isabella possesses qualities I lack, understanding I'll never achieve, belonging I can never earn no matter how successful my business becomes.

"I should check on dinner service," I say, desperate to escape before tears betray me.

"Of course, dear. I'm sure you have a thousand details to manage." Mrs. Judd's smile is kind, which somehow makes it worse. "But Lianne? Before you go?"

I force myself to meet her eyes.

"I hope you know I'm not saying this to be unkind. I've watched you work tonight, and you're clearly exceptional at what you do. Truly gifted." She pauses, her voice dropping to something that might be genuine kindness or perfectly executed cruelty—I can't tell anymore. "But sometimes the kindest thing we can do for people we care about is to be honest about reality. You understand, don't you? Some situations require clarity for everyone's well-being."

"I understand completely," I say, my voice barely steady. "Thank you for sharing your perspective, Mrs. Judd."

I escape toward the kitchen before she can say anything else, before the tears building behind my eyes can fall where anyone might see them. In the service corridor, I lean against the wall and try to breathe through the crushing pressure in my chest.

She knows. She figured it out. And her response wasn't anger or confrontation—it was worse. It was polite dismissal dressed as compliment, acknowledgment of my success paired with clear delineation of my limits.

You're talented, but you'll never be enough. You've achieved something impressive, but you still don't belong. You can plan their events, but you'll never be welcome at their table.

Through the service window, I watch guests moving toward their assigned tables. Cameron escorts Isabella to Table One, pulling out her chair with gallant attention while she accepts with natural grace, her smile radiant and comfortable. They settle into conversation easily, the kind of effortless interaction that requires no effort because they're from the same world, speak the same language, understand the same unspoken rules.

Mrs. Judd joins them, her expression pleased as she watches her son with the woman she's chosen for him. The woman who understands what's expected. The woman who won't complicate his life with incompatible backgrounds or inconvenient emotions.

They belong there. Together, at that table, in this world I've spent the evening perfecting but will never inhabit as anything more than staff.

As dinner service begins with military precision—the result of weeks of planning and coordination—I retreat to my position behind the scenes, managing the evening's logistics while remaining invisible to the guests enjoying the fruits of my labor.

This is where I belong. Managing the magic while others live it. Creating experiences for people who will never see me as more than the help, no matter how exceptional my work might be.

Tonight will be perfect. Every detail flawless. Every moment exactly as planned.

But for me, it's goodbye.

17

Cameron

THE GALA ENDS at midnight with speeches and toasts celebrating fifty years of Sterling Industries. I barely hear my own words as I announce the scholarship program—the one Lianne helped design, the one that was supposed to show her I've changed.

Everything is perfect. Everyone is satisfied. Industry contacts are already praising the execution.

But all I can see is Lianne coordinating from the shadows, her face carefully blank, maintaining professional distance that feels like a chasm I can't cross.

Guests filter out in clusters, calling for valets, making plans to continue celebrations at the hotel bar. I watch Lianne supervising the breakdown crew with the same meticulous attention she's brought to every detail tonight, and I know something is desperately wrong.

"Lianne."

She doesn't turn around, her clipboard clutched like armor. "The event was a success. Your guests were happy.

The industry feedback has been outstanding. That's what matters."

"Stop it." My voice comes out rougher than intended, frustration and fear making it harsh. "Stop hiding behind professional courtesy. Something's been wrong all night. Talk to me."

She finally faces me, and what I see steals my breath. She looks like she's already said goodbye, like she's already mourned us and moved on while I'm still trying to hold on.

Behind her, through the ballroom windows, I can see my mother and Isabella still talking, both looking pleased with how the evening went. But that's not what this is about— Isabella made it clear weeks ago she's not interested, and I've barely spoken to her all night beyond polite pleasantries.

"What's happening is that I'm remembering why this can't work," Lianne says quietly, each word precise and devastating. "Your mother was right. I watched it all night— watched you with your family, with your world. And I finally understood what she was trying to tell me."

"What are you talking about?" Panic edges into my voice.

"At the gala six months ago, your mother told me something I didn't want to hear." Her voice shakes despite her obvious effort to stay controlled. "She said Isabella understands your world in ways I never will. That she can be a real partner in all aspects of your life. And tonight, watching you move through this room with such ease, seeing how naturally you belong here—"

"Lianne, Isabella has a boyfriend in Milan. You know that. This isn't about her."

"It's not about Isabella specifically." She sets down her clipboard with trembling hands. "It's about what she represents. Someone who doesn't have to learn your world from scratch, who doesn't feel like an imposter at every family dinner, who doesn't spend half her energy trying to figure out which fork to use or what the unspoken rules are."

"That's not—"

"I've been lying to myself, Cameron." Tears finally spill over. "Telling myself that if I just worked hard enough, if I built a successful enough business, if I proved myself valuable enough, then maybe I could belong. But tonight, watching you with your family, seeing how easily you navigate their world—I realized I'll never truly fit. And I'm exhausted from pretending that doesn't matter."

The words hit like physical blows. "You do fit. You belong with me."

"Do I?" Her laugh is bitter, broken. "I coordinated your family's celebration tonight. I made sure everything was perfect for them. But I didn't belong at those tables, Cameron. I was the help—and that's fine, that's my job. But it made me realize something."

She takes a shuddering breath. "Even when I'm not working, even at family dinners or social events, part of me is always performing. Always hyperaware that I'm different, that I came from nothing, that your world has rules I'll never instinctively understand because I wasn't born into it."

"That doesn't matter to me. It never has."

"But it matters to me!" The admission tears out of her. "It matters that I spend every interaction with your family analyzing whether I'm doing it right, whether I'm using the correct terminology, whether my success is impressive enough to make up for my background. It matters that I'll always be the foster kid who got lucky, not someone who naturally belongs in rooms like this."

Through the windows, I see my mother glancing our way, her expression shifting from satisfaction to concern as she reads the tension in our body language.

"Your mother tried to warn me," Lianne continues, her voice dropping to something raw and vulnerable. "She was actually being kind, in her way. Trying to help me understand what I was getting into before I got hurt. And I was so angry at her for it, but she was right."

"She was wrong," I say desperately. "She doesn't get to define what you're capable of or where you belong."

"She wasn't defining what I'm capable of. She was acknowledging a reality I've been refusing to see." Lianne's face crumples, years of carefully buried insecurity finally breaking through. "I don't belong in your world, Cameron. Not because I'm not good enough or successful enough, but because it's not my world. It never will be. And I'm tired of fighting to fit into a place that doesn't want me."

"I want you. That's all that matters."

"Is it?" She looks at me with such devastating sadness. "What about when we have children and your mother wants them in the right schools with the right connections? What about when your business associates wonder why you married the event planner instead of someone from your own circle? What about all the thousand tiny moments when I'll be reminded that I don't quite fit?"

"We'll face those moments together."

"But I'll face them alone in my head, Cameron. Every single time, I'll be the one wondering if I'm enough, if I belong, if you'll eventually realize your mother was right."

Her voice breaks completely. "I can't spend my life waiting for you to figure out what everyone else already knows—that someone from your world would be easier."

"I don't want easier. I want you."

"You say that now." She picks up her coordination folder with hands that won't stop shaking. "But your mother was trying to save us both from the inevitable. From the moment when you realize that loving me means constantly explaining me, defending me, bridging worlds that shouldn't need bridging."

I reach for her, desperate, but she steps back like my touch would shatter what's left of her composure.

"Don't. Please don't make this harder than it already is."

"I'm not letting you go. Not when these are just fears talking, not reality."

"They're not just fears." Professional armor snaps back into place, but I can see it's brittle, ready to shatter. "They're the truth I've been avoiding because I wanted so badly to believe that love was enough. But it's not, Cameron. Love doesn't erase the fact that I'll always be uncomfortable in your world. That I'll always feel like I'm performing rather than belonging."

She forces herself to meet my eyes one last time. "I can't be the woman you love in private while feeling like an imposter in public. I can't spend my life wondering when you'll see what your mother sees—that I'm impressive for someone from my background, but my background disqualifies me from your future."

"That's not going to happen."

"It already has." She picks up her things with a finality that terrifies me. "I felt it tonight, watching myself coordinate while your family celebrated. Feeling the difference between who I am and where you come from. Your mother knew it six months ago. I just finally accepted it."

"Lianne, please—"

"Thank you for choosing Luminous Events for this celebration." Her voice is professionally neutral, each word carefully controlled. "We'll send the final invoice next week. I hope the evening met all of Sterling Industries' objectives."

The formal words feel like a door slamming shut.

"This isn't about the event. This is about us."

"There is no us." Tears stream down her face even as she maintains that terrible professional composure. "There's you in your world, and me in mine, and I finally understand that trying to bridge them was always going to end this way. With me exhausted from pretending I belong somewhere I never will."

She walks away, and this time I let her go because I can see that holding on will only hurt her more. I watch her coordinate the breakdown with her team, maintaining professional composure even as I can see her heart breaking.

Amanda catches her expression and says something I can't hear. Lianne forces a smile and keeps working, keeps functioning, keeps surviving because that's what she does.

Through the windows, I see my mother approaching, Isabella at her side.

The rage that's been building since Lianne walked away finally finds its target.

"Cameron, darling, what a successful evening," my mother begins, her voice warm with satisfaction. "Everyone is talking about how spectacular—"

"What did you say to her?" I cut her off, my voice cold in a way she's never heard from me.

My mother blinks, momentarily thrown. "I'm sorry, what?"

"Lianne. What did you say to Lianne six months ago at the first gala?"

Isabella shifts uncomfortably, clearly sensing this is about to get ugly. "I should go find my parents—"

"Stay," I say, my eyes never leaving my mother. "This concerns you too."

My mother's expression shifts from confusion to calculated innocence. "I simply complimented her on the beautiful event, Cameron. She's clearly very talented at what she does."

"And what else?"

A pause. "I may have mentioned that it's wonderful to see you spending time with someone from your own world. Someone who understands—"

"Someone who understands what?" I step closer, my voice dropping to something dangerous. "Someone whose family has the right connections? Someone whose background doesn't require explanation?"

"Cameron, I don't appreciate your tone—"

"And I don't appreciate you interfering in my personal life." The words come out sharp, final. "You told Lianne she was talented but ultimately inappropriate. That Isabella would be a better match because her family understands the responsibilities that come with my position."

Isabella makes a small sound of distress. "Mrs. Judd, you didn't—"

"I was simply being honest about reality," my mother

says, her voice taking on steel. "Cameron has responsibilities, expectations. He needs a partner who can navigate—"

"What I need," I interrupt, my voice carrying across the nearly empty ballroom, "is for my family to stop trying to orchestrate my life like it's a business merger."

My father appears from wherever he's been networking. "Cameron, what's going on?"

"Mother just drove away the woman I love by telling her she's not good enough for our family." I turn to face both of them, making sure they understand I'm done playing their games. "That she's talented and accomplished, but her background disqualifies her from being with me."

"That's not what I said," my mother protests, but there's guilt in her expression now.

"Isn't it?" I challenge. "You told her Isabella understands my world in ways Lianne never will. That Isabella can be a real partner in all aspects of my life. That her family understands the responsibilities that come with wealth and position."

Isabella steps forward, her voice firm despite obvious discomfort. "Mr. and Mrs. Judd, I need to be clear about something. I'm not interested in Cameron romantically. I never have been. I came tonight as a family friend, nothing more."

My mother's mouth opens in shock.

"I'm actually in a relationship with someone in Milan," Isabella continues. "I mentioned this to you, Mrs. Judd, but you seemed to... overlook it. I care about Cameron, but only as a friend. Whatever matchmaking you had in mind, it's not going to happen."

My father looks between all of us, finally understanding the situation. "Eleanor, what did you do?"

"I was trying to help." My mother's voice wavers. "Cameron deserves someone who—"

"Cameron deserves to make his own choices," I cut her off. "I'm thirty years old. I've built Sterling Industries into something that matters, created impact beyond just profit margins, proven I don't need your money or your connections to succeed. And I'm done letting you dictate who I can love."

"You dated her four years ago," my mother says, desperation creeping in. "It didn't work then. What makes you think—"

"It didn't work because I was too weak to stand up to you." The admission tastes like failure. "Because I let your disapproval matter more than her happiness. Because I chose the easy path instead of fighting for what we had."

"Cameron—"

"I love her, Mother. I love Lianne Peralta. The event planner who came from foster care and built a successful company through talent and determination. The woman who's more accomplished at thirty than most people with trust funds and connections ever achieve. The woman who taught me that privilege is a responsibility, not a birthright."

My mother looks stricken. "I only want what's best for you."

"Then want me to be happy." My voice softens slightly, but the steel remains. "Want me to be with someone who challenges me and inspires me and makes me want to be better than I am. That's Lianne. Not Isabella, not whoever else you want to parade in front of me. Lianne."

"But her background—"

"Is exactly why she's extraordinary." I cut off that line of argument permanently. "She succeeded without the advantages we take for granted. She built something meaningful without family money or connections. She earned every single thing she has, which is more than either of us can say."

My father clears his throat. "Cameron's right, Eleanor. We've been... overstepping."

My mother looks between us, tears forming. "I just wanted to protect you from making a mistake."

"Letting her go was the mistake." I force myself to say it, to own it. "Four years ago, I made the biggest mistake of my life because I cared more about your approval than her happiness. I'm not making that mistake again."

"What are you saying?"

"I'm saying that if you can't accept Lianne, you'll see a lot less of me." The ultimatum hangs in the air. "I'll still be board chair of Sterling Industries. I'll still attend family obligations. But I won't pretend my personal life is up for committee review."

"You're choosing her over your family?" My mother's voice breaks.

"I'm choosing myself," I correct. "I'm choosing to be with someone who makes me happy instead of someone who makes you comfortable. If you can't support that, I understand. But I'm done compromising on this."

Silence stretches across the ballroom. Isabella has quietly excused herself, leaving just the three of us and the ruins of their expectations.

"She's already gone," my mother says quietly. "I saw her leave. You might be too late."

"I know." The pain of watching Lianne walk away is still fresh. "But I need you to understand that whether or not she gives me another chance, this ends tonight. Your interference in my personal life, your matchmaking attempts, your subtle suggestions about who I should date. All of it stops."

My father nods slowly. "That's fair. We've been... we haven't respected your autonomy the way we should."

"Eleanor?" I look at my mother, waiting.

She wipes her eyes, her composure cracking for the first time I can remember. "I just wanted you to have an easier path than loving someone the world might not understand."

"I know. But easy isn't always right." I soften slightly, seeing her genuine distress. "I love you both. But I love her too. And I need you to respect that."

My mother nods shakily. "If she makes you happy..."

"She does. She makes me want to be someone worthy of her."

"Then I suppose..." She takes a breath. "I suppose I owe her an apology. A real one."

"You do. But not tonight." I look toward where Lianne's team is finishing the breakdown. "Tonight, I need to figure out how to fix what we broke."

"Go," my father says. "We'll talk more tomorrow."

I don't wait for my mother's approval. I head toward the exit, pulling out my phone, knowing I probably can't fix this tonight but needing to try anyway.

Because Lianne deserves to know that I finally stood up to my family.

That I finally chose her.

Even if I'm too late to make it matter.

18

———

Lianne

A week later

I SHOULD BE CELEBRATING.

Los Angeles Magazine called the Sterling Industries gala "the gold standard for luxury corporate celebrations." The article features a full-page spread of the ballroom, the peonies catching light just perfectly, guests in elegant clusters that suggest the kind of effortless sophistication that takes months to orchestrate.

Three Fortune 500 companies have inquired about hiring us. The phone hasn't stopped ringing with referrals—tech moguls wanting anniversary celebrations, nonprofits seeking gala coordination, wealthy families planning weddings that require the kind of discretion and excellence we've now proven we can deliver.

It's everything I dreamed of when I started Luminous Events. The kind of success that validates every eighteen-hour day, every impossible client, every moment I doubted whether I could actually build something that mattered.

Yet here I am, six days after the gala, surrounded by vendor contracts and timeline proposals, using work as armor against the pain sitting in my chest like a stone that grows heavier every time I stop moving.

"The Martinez wedding photos are ready," Amanda says, appearing in my doorway with her tablet and the concerned expression she's been wearing all week. "Maria and Carlos want to schedule a review session. They're excited to see everything."

"Next week," I say without looking up from the Highland Community Center proposal I'm reviewing for the third time, the words blurring together because I can't actually focus enough to absorb them.

"You said that yesterday. And the day before." Amanda doesn't leave, just stands there radiating worry. "You're already booked solid for the next two weeks. Plus you added that Highland fundraiser and two venue visits that weren't on yesterday's calendar. You're filling every available hour with work."

"We have momentum to capitalize on. The Sterling gala opened doors we need to walk through while the industry attention is fresh." The explanation sounds hollow even to my own ears.

Amanda sets down her tablet with a soft thud that demands attention. "Cameron called three times Sunday trying to reach you. He left messages saying he needed to talk to you, that he stood up to his family, that he chose you."

My chest tightens with something between longing and panic. "What did you tell him?"

"That you weren't available. That you'd call him back when you had time." Amanda's voice softens. "But Lianne, he sounded devastated. And then Monday morning his assistant called to say he had to fly to Frankfurt for emergency meetings about the renewable energy acquisition. That he'd be gone all week but he wanted you to know he'd keep trying to reach you when he got back."

So he's in Europe. That explains why the calls stopped after Monday, why there's been radio silence except for the occasional text that appears at odd hours—time zone differences making his 2 AM my 5 PM.

I pull up my phone and scroll through the messages I haven't responded to:

Sunday, 11:47 PM: Please call me. I need to tell you what happened after you left. I stood up to my family. I chose you.

Monday, 6:23 AM: I have to fly to Frankfurt for the week. Emergency meetings I can't postpone. But I'm not giving up on us. Please, just think about what I said.

Tuesday, 2:14 AM (9:14 AM Frankfurt time): I know you're avoiding me and I understand why. But Lianne, this isn't about my family anymore. I finally understand what the real problem is.

Wednesday, 3:47 AM: Missing you. Thinking about you. Wishing I could make you see yourself the way I see you.

Thursday, 1:32 AM: I get back Saturday. Can we please talk? Just give me one chance to explain what I finally understand.

Friday, 2:58 AM: One more day. Then I'm coming home to fight for us. Because you're worth fighting for, even if you don't believe that yet.

Each message is restrained, respectful of my space, but

threaded with desperation that makes my throat tight. He's not begging or demanding—he's just... there. Persistent but not pushy. Waiting but not giving up.

"You haven't responded to any of them, have you?" Amanda asks, reading my expression.

"What would I say?" The question comes out more broken than intended. "That I'm sorry I walked away because I was too scared to believe I deserved him? That I destroyed something beautiful because my trauma convinced me it couldn't last?"

"Yes," Amanda says simply. "That's exactly what you should say."

Before I can respond, my door opens without warning and Maya walks in carrying coffee and the determined expression of someone who's been summoned for an intervention.

"Amanda called me," Maya says without preamble, setting a latte in front of me—my usual order, the one I haven't had time to get myself this week. "She's worried you're having a breakdown disguised as productivity."

I glare at Amanda, who has the grace to look only mildly apologetic.

"When's the last time you left this office for something other than business?" Maya settles into the chair beside Amanda, creating a united front. "When's the last time you ate a real meal, or slept more than four hours, or did anything that wasn't directly related to event planning?"

I can't remember. The days since Saturday have blurred together in a haze of contract reviews, vendor coordination, and strategic planning sessions designed to keep my mind occupied and my heart safely locked away behind professional competence.

"I'm fine," I say, but the words sound unconvincing even to me.

"You're not fine. You're barely functional." Maya leans forward, her voice dropping to something softer. "You're hiding, Lianne. You're scared of dealing with what happened Saturday night, so you're working yourself to exhaustion to avoid having feelings you can't control."

The observation hits too close to home. Because she's right—I've been terrified. Terrified of the hurt that threatens to overwhelm me every time I stop coordinating and planning and executing. Terrified of examining what happened, of acknowledging that I'm the one who walked away, that my own fears destroyed something beautiful.

"What happened Saturday wasn't Cameron's fault," I whisper. "It was mine."

"I know," Maya says gently. "And I think you know it too. That's why you're avoiding him—because if you talk to him, you'll have to admit that you're the one who sabotaged things. That you left him because you were scared, not because he failed you."

Tears blur my vision. "His mother told me I'd never belong in his world. And she was right—I don't. I'll always be the foster kid performing, always wondering if I'm using the right fork or saying the right thing or—"

"Stop." Maya's voice is firm. "Just stop. You know what you're doing? You're letting Vivian Judd—a woman who's never had to earn anything in her life—define your worth. You're letting her casual cruelty become your internal truth."

"But what if she's right? What if I really can't—"

"Can't what? Navigate social situations? You coordinate events for the wealthiest people in Los Angeles. You read rooms better than anyone I know. You anticipate needs before people know they have them." Maya's expression softens. "The only person who thinks you don't belong in Cameron's world is you. And that's not reality, Lianne. That's trauma."

The word hangs in the air between us.

Trauma.

"I've been reading about attachment styles," Maya continues carefully. "About how foster kids develop patterns of leaving before they can be left. Of sabotaging relationships when they get too good because deep down, they don't believe good things can last."

My hands shake as I set down my coffee cup. "That's what I did. That's exactly what I did."

"I know. And Cameron knows it too—that's what his texts have been trying to tell you. He's not upset that you left. He's devastated that you don't believe you deserve to be loved." Maya reaches across the desk to take my hand. "But here's the thing about trauma patterns—recognizing them is the first step to changing them."

"What if I can't change? What if I'm always going to feel this way?"

"Then you work on it. You get therapy, you talk to Cameron about your fears when they come up, you learn to recognize when your brain is lying to you about not deserving good things." She squeezes my hand. "But you don't run away from someone who loves you because you're scared. That's letting the trauma win."

Amanda clears her throat. "For what it's worth, I've

watched Cameron around you. The way he looks at you, the way he talks about you when you're not there—that man is completely gone for you. And I don't think he cares whether you know which fork to use."

"He stood up to his family for me," I say quietly. "Sunday night, after I left. He told them he loves me and they need to accept it or see less of him."

"He told you that?" Maya asks.

"In his texts. He's been trying to tell me all week." I pull up the messages again, reading them with new eyes. "He keeps saying he finally understands what the real problem is. I thought he meant his family, but..."

"But he means your inability to believe you deserve him," Maya finishes. "Which is actually much more insightful than just throwing grand gestures at the problem."

Silence settles over my office as I process what they're saying. That Cameron isn't the problem. His family isn't the problem. The problem is me—or more specifically, the scared little girl inside me who learned early that belonging was temporary, that love was conditional, that eventually everyone sees something wrong with you and sends you away.

"He gets back Saturday," I say, looking at his last message. "What do I do?"

"You decide whether you're brave enough to fight for something good," Maya says simply. "Whether you're willing to risk being hurt for the possibility of being happy. Because that's what this comes down to—are you going to let fear make your decisions, or are you going to choose love even though it's terrifying?"

After they leave, I sit alone with those questions echoing in my mind.

Am I brave enough? Can I fight my own trauma patterns? Can I believe I deserve good things even when my entire childhood taught me otherwise?

I pull out my phone and look at Cameron's messages again. Each one carefully worded to give me space while making clear he's not giving up. Each one showing he understands this is about my fears, not his failures.

I finally understand what the real problem is.

He gets it. He understands that this isn't about his family or Isabella or public declarations. He understands that the enemy isn't external—it's the voice in my head telling me I don't belong.

I open a new message and stare at the blank screen for a long time.

Finally, I type:

ME:

> I'm scared. I'm terrified of believing this can work when my whole life has taught me that I'm temporary. But I think I'm more scared of losing you because I was too afraid to try. When you get back, can we talk?

I hit send before I can second-guess myself.

The response comes almost immediately—must be evening in Frankfurt.

CAMERON:

> Yes. God, yes. I land Saturday at 2pm. I'll come straight to you.

ME:

No. Let me come to you. Tell me where.

There's a longer pause this time. Then:

CAMERON:

My place in Malibu. I'll text you the address.

ME:

Ok

CAMERON:

Thank you for being brave enough to reach
out. I know how hard that is for you.

The fact that he recognizes the courage it took—that he understands how much my trauma makes reaching out feel like risking everything—makes tears spill over.

ME:

See you Saturday.

I set down my phone and take my first deep breath in six days.

This isn't fixed. One conversation won't undo thirty years of believing I don't deserve good things. But it's a start.

For the first time in my life, I'm choosing to reach out instead of running away.

I'm choosing to fight for something good, even though it terrifies me.

I'm choosing love over fear.

And maybe that's what healing looks like—not the absence of fear, but the decision to be brave anyway.

.   .   .

Saturday morning, I wake up to panic.

What am I doing? What was I thinking? Cameron Judd lives in Malibu in a house I've never seen, in a world I'll never fully belong to. His mother was right—someone like Isabella would be easier for him. Someone who doesn't come with trauma and baggage and a lifetime of reasons to believe she's not enough.

I reach for my phone to cancel, to tell him I made a mistake.

But then I see Maya's text from last night:

MAYA:

Remember—the scared voice isn't the truth. It's just your trauma trying to protect you the only way it knows how. You're brave enough for this. I believe in you even if you don't believe in yourself yet.

I read it three times, letting the words sink in.

The scared voice isn't the truth.

My hands are shaking as I get ready. I change outfits four times before settling on jeans and a simple white blouse— casual but put-together, the kind of outfit that says I'm not trying too hard but I care about this moment.

The drive to Malibu takes forty-five minutes through Saturday morning traffic. Cameron's address leads me to a private road that winds up through hills, past estates with ocean views and gates that suggest serious money. His house sits at the end of the road, a modern structure of glass and natural wood that somehow manages to feel both impressive and welcoming.

I park in the circular driveway next to his Aston Martin

and just sit for a moment, my heart pounding so hard I can hear it.

I could still leave. Could text him that I'm not ready, that I need more time. Could let fear win one more time.

Instead, I get out of the car and walk to his front door.

Before I can ring the bell, the door opens. Cameron stands there in jeans and a T-shirt, his hair still damp from a shower, his expression equal parts hope and terror.

"You came," he says, like he wasn't entirely sure I would.

"I came." My voice shakes despite my best efforts. "Can I... can we talk?"

"Of course. Come in." He steps back to let me enter.

The house is beautiful—open floor plan with floor-to-ceiling windows showcasing the Pacific, comfortable furniture that looks actually lived-in rather than just expensive, personal touches that make it feel like a home rather than a showpiece. Family photos on the mantle. Books on the shelves. A piano in the corner that shows signs of regular use.

"This is beautiful," I say, needing to fill the silence.

"Thank you. Can I get you something? Coffee? Water?"

"Water would be good."

He disappears into the kitchen, giving me a moment to breathe. When he returns with two glasses, his hands are shaking slightly.

We settle on the couch facing the ocean, close enough to talk but far enough apart that we're not touching.

"I'm glad you reached out," Cameron says finally. "I wasn't sure you would."

"I almost didn't." The admission slips out before I can stop it. "I woke up this morning convinced this was a mistake. That I should cancel, stay home, let you move on with your life."

"What changed your mind?"

"My best friend told me that the scared voice isn't the truth. That it's just my trauma trying to protect me." I take a sip of water, needing the moment to gather courage. "And I realized she was right. That I've been letting fear make my decisions my entire life. Running away before I can be rejected. Leaving before I can be left."

Cameron sets down his glass, his full attention on me. "Lianne—"

"Please, let me say this before I lose my nerve." I force myself to meet his eyes. "What happened at the gala wasn't your fault. You didn't do anything wrong. Your family wasn't the problem. The problem was me—or more specifically, the scared little girl inside me who's spent thirty years learning that she doesn't belong anywhere."

"You belong with me," he says quietly.

"Maybe. But I need you to understand something." I take a shaky breath. "I'm always going to have moments where I feel like I'm performing. Where I wonder if I'm using the right fork or saying the right thing or if I'm good enough to be in your world. That's not going to just disappear because we have one conversation."

"I know."

"And your mother's words—they didn't create these fears. They just confirmed what I already believed about myself." Tears blur my vision. "That I'm talented for someone from my background. That I've achieved something impressive considering where I came from. But that my background disqualifies me from your future."

Cameron shifts closer, his hand hovering near mine but not quite touching. "Can I tell you what I see when I look at you?"

I nod, not trusting my voice.

"I see someone who built an empire from nothing. Who took every disadvantage she was handed and turned it into strength. Who's more accomplished at thirty than most people with trust funds and connections ever achieve." His voice is fierce with conviction. "I see someone who's brilliant at reading people, who creates magic for others, who makes every room better just by being in it."

"Cameron—"

"I see someone who thinks she's performing at family dinners when she's actually just being herself—thoughtful, interesting, engaged. Someone who thinks she's using the wrong fork when nobody else is even paying attention to forks because they're too busy enjoying her company."

The tears spill over. "What if you're wrong? What if I really am just—"

"Just what? Not good enough?" He finally takes my hand, his touch warm and steady. "Lianne, the only person who thinks that is you. And I finally understand—this isn't something I can fix by standing up to my family or making public declarations. This is something you have to work through yourself."

"I know," I whisper. "Maya suggested therapy. Said I need to learn to recognize when my trauma is lying to me about deserving good things."

"I think that's a good idea. And I want to support you through that however I can." He pauses. "But I need you to understand something too. I'm not giving up on us. Even when you're scared, even when you want to run, even when your trauma tells you this can't last—I'm choosing you. Every single day, I'm choosing you."

"What if I can't change? What if I'm always going to feel like this?"

"Then we'll deal with it together. We'll create a code word for when your fears are talking instead of reality. We'll talk about it when you're feeling like you don't belong. We'll work through it as a team instead of you suffering alone."

The offer—to not have to face this alone, to have someone who understands and wants to help rather than just getting frustrated—breaks something open in my chest.

"I'm so sorry," I sob. "I'm so sorry I walked away. That I let my fears destroy something beautiful before it even had a real chance."

"Hey, look at me." Cameron cups my face, his thumbs brushing away tears. "You're here now. You reached out even though it terrified you. You're choosing to fight for us instead of running away. That's what matters."

"I'm scared," I admit. "I'm terrified this won't work. That eventually you'll realize your mother was right, that someone from your world would be easier."

"Easier isn't better. And I don't want someone from my world—I want you. Complicated, beautiful, traumatized, brilliant you." He leans his forehead against mine. "We'll figure this out together. One day at a time, one fear at a time, one moment at a time when you're brave enough to believe you deserve good things."

"I want to believe that," I whisper. "I want to believe I can do this."

"Then start with right now. Right now, in this moment, can you believe that I love you?"

I look into his eyes—hazel with gold flecks, completely focused on me like I'm the only thing that matters in his world. And in this moment, I can believe it. I can feel it in how he's holding me, in how he's been waiting for me, in how he understands this is about my trauma rather than his failures.

"Yes," I say. "Right now, I can believe it."

"Good. That's enough for today. Tomorrow we'll work on believing it then too." He kisses my forehead gently. "Baby steps. That's all we need—baby steps toward trusting that you deserve good things."

We sit there for a long time, holding each other while the Pacific sparkles beyond his windows. It's not fixed—I know that. One conversation doesn't undo thirty years of trauma. But it's a beginning.

For the first time in my life, I'm not running away.

I'm staying. I'm fighting. I'm choosing love even though it terrifies me.

And maybe that's enough for now.

19

Cameron

THREE MONTHS LATER, I watch Lianne coordinate the Highland Community Center fundraiser with the same meticulous attention she brings to every event, but there's something different about her tonight.

She's relaxed in a way I haven't seen before. Laughing easily with volunteers, handling minor crises with grace, moving through the space like she belongs here rather than performing belonging.

"She looks happy," Maya says, appearing at my elbow with two glasses of wine. "Really happy. Not performing-happy, but genuine."

"She is." I accept the wine gratefully. "The therapy is helping. She's learning to recognize when her trauma is lying to her."

"And you're being patient with the process."

"Of course. She's worth it." I watch Lianne crouch down to talk to a little girl, probably seven or eight, making the child laugh with something she says. "Every moment of patience, every difficult conversation, every time I have to reassure her that she deserves good things—it's worth it to see her like this."

The fundraiser is spectacular—exactly what Lianne envisioned when she proposed it three months ago. The community center transformed into an elegant celebration space, live music from local artists, food from Filipino restaurants she specifically selected, auction items that will raise serious money for their programs.

But the real magic is in the details that show how much this place matters to her. Photo displays showing kids from the foster system who succeeded. Stories from program participants. Information about the scholarship fund we created—the one that bears her name now, because she finally stopped protesting that she didn't deserve that honor.

"Speech in five minutes," Amanda announces, appearing with her tablet. "Cameron, you're introducing Lianne. She's doing the main program update."

"Got it." I down the rest of my wine and head toward the small stage.

The crowd quiets as I step up to the microphone. Familiar faces from our combined worlds—Sterling Industries board members mixing with Highland Community Center volunteers, my family sitting with Maya and Declan, Lianne's Luminous Events team scattered throughout.

"Good evening, everyone. Thank you for being here tonight to support an organization that changes lives." I find Lianne in the crowd, and she gives me an encouraging smile. "Three months ago, the woman I love challenged me to think about privilege differently. Not as something to maintain or protect, but as a responsibility to create opportunities for others."

I see Lianne's expression shift—surprise mixed with emotion.

"Lianne Peralta grew up in the foster system. She aged out with no family, no safety net, no advantages beyond her own determination and talent. And she built something extraordinary anyway." I pause, making sure I have everyone's attention. "But she never forgot where she came from. She never stopped believing that kids like her deserve better support, better opportunities, better chances to succeed."

The crowd is completely silent now.

"So when we started dating, she didn't just accept my world—she challenged it. Made me question what I was doing with my privilege, whether I was using it to create real impact or just maintain status quo." I find my mother in the crowd, and she nods, tears in her eyes. "Tonight's fundraiser exists because Lianne believed this community deserved investment. Because she fought for funding, created partnerships, leveraged her industry connections to make this happen."

I gesture toward the displays. "The scholarship program you see documented here has already helped fifteen kids pursue careers in hospitality and business. By next year, we hope to triple that number. And it's all because one woman refused to forget where she came from, even as she built an empire."

Applause starts, building to something overwhelming.

"Please join me in welcoming the woman who made tonight possible—Lianne Peralta."

She walks to the stage looking nervous but determined.

When she reaches me, I kiss her cheek and whisper, "You've got this."

"Thank you, Cameron." She turns to the crowd, taking a deep breath. "Three months ago, I stood in this community center feeling like I'd come home. This is where I spent time as a teenager, where counselors helped me figure out college applications and job interviews and all the practical skills you need when you don't have family to teach you."

Her voice is steady now, confident.

"I was terrified to get involved with this fundraiser. Terrified of facing the parts of my past I usually keep private. But someone I love very much taught me that hiding from your past gives it more power than it deserves." She looks at me, and I can see the work she's done to get here, to stand in front of everyone and own her story. "So instead of hiding, I decided to use my past to create better futures for other kids."

She talks about the scholarship program, about the partnerships with event planning companies who've committed to hiring program participants, about the mentorship initiative pairing successful professionals with kids aging out of the system.

But what strikes me most is how she owns her story without shame. How she talks about foster care not as something to be pitied but as part of what made her who she is—resilient, determined, unwilling to accept that background determines destiny.

This is the woman I fell in love with. Not performing, not trying to prove anything. Just completely herself.

After her speech, after the auction wraps up, after we've thanked every volunteer and donor and supporter, we finally escape to the parking lot where her car and mine are parked side by side.

"That was incredible," I say, pulling her close. "You were incredible."

"I only cried twice during the speech," she says, laughing. "That's progress, right?"

"Huge progress. Three months ago, you wouldn't have even agreed to speak."

"Three months ago, I was convinced I had to hide where I came from to deserve being with you." She reaches up to cup my face. "Thank you for being patient while I figured out that was my trauma talking."

"Always. Though I have to admit, watching you own your story tonight—seeing you completely comfortable in your own skin—that's the sexiest thing I've ever seen."

She laughs, bright and unguarded. "Sexier than the time I wore that red dress to your company party?"

"Much sexier. That was just physical attraction. This is being completely gone for every part of you, including the parts you used to think were weaknesses."

"I love you," she says, and there's no hesitation in it now, no fear that saying it means risking too much.

"I love you too. Come home with me?"

"Your place or mine?"

"Mine. I want to wake up with you looking at the ocean."

"Deal. But I'm driving separately—I have an early vendor meeting tomorrow."

"Of course you do." I kiss her thoroughly, not caring that volunteers are still milling around, that Amanda is probably watching with knowing amusement, that my mother is definitely taking photos.

This is who we are now—public, permanent, completely committed to making this work despite the challenges.

Later, at my place in Malibu, we sit on the deck watching moonlight on the Pacific.

"I've been thinking," Lianne says, her head resting on my shoulder. "About what comes next."

"What do you mean?"

"I mean us. Where this is going." She shifts to face me. "I know we're taking things slow, being careful with my trauma patterns. But Cameron, I don't want to spend the rest of my life just managing my fears. I want to build something with you."

My heart rate picks up. "What are you saying?"

"I'm saying that therapy has helped me understand that I'll always have moments where I'm scared. Where my trauma tells me I don't deserve good things or that this won't last." She takes my hand. "But those moments are getting smaller. Quieter. Easier to recognize as fear rather than reality."

"That's incredible progress."

"And I've realized something else. Waiting until I'm completely healed before we move forward is just another way of letting fear control my life." Her eyes are bright with determination. "So I'm choosing to be brave. To build a future with you even though part of me is still scared."

"Lianne, what are you asking?"

"I'm asking if you want to move in together. Officially, not just me sleeping over most nights." She laughs nervously. "I know it's fast, but also we've known each other for four years, dated twice, and I think I'm finally ready to trust that this is real."

I pull her into my lap, framing her face with my hands. "Yes. God, yes. I've been waiting for you to be ready."

"Really? You're not worried it's too soon?"

"Lianne, I've known I wanted to spend my life with you since the first time around. The only question was whether you'd believe you deserved that." I kiss her softly. "The fact that you're choosing to be brave, to trust this despite your fears—that's everything I've been hoping for."

"I'm still going to have bad days," she warns. "Days where my trauma tells me I don't belong, where I want to run away because things feel too good."

"I know. And on those days, we'll use our code word. We'll talk about it. We'll get through it together." I brush hair from her face. "That's what partners do—they show up for each other's hard moments, not just the easy ones."

"When did you get so wise?"

"When I fell in love with a woman who challenged me to be better than I was. Who taught me that real love means supporting someone through their healing, not just enjoying them when they're healed."

She kisses me then, deep and thorough, and I taste promise in it. Not perfection—we're both too aware of the work ahead for that—but commitment. Partnership. The decision to choose each other even when it's difficult.

"My place or yours?" I ask when we finally break apart.

"Let's start with yours. It's bigger, better for when we're both working from home." She pauses. "But eventually, I'd like to find something that's ours. A place we choose together."

"I like that idea. Something that represents both of us."

"With space for your piano and my event planning chaos."

"And a guest room for when my family visits, since apparently my mother has decided you're her favorite person now."

Lianne laughs at that. "She's been surprisingly supportive since her apology. Last week she invited me to her book club again. I think she's genuinely trying."

"She is. You terrified her at first—challenged everything she believed about who belonged in our world. But she's learning that belonging isn't about bloodlines or background. It's about character and capability and courage."

"Courage," Lianne repeats. "I like that. Because it does take courage to believe I deserve this. To trust that you're not going to wake up one day and realize your mother was right."

"She wasn't right. She was projecting her own insecurities about what it means to be worthy." I pull Lianne closer. "And you've taught our whole family something valuable— that success earned is more impressive than success inherited. That resilience built through hardship is stronger than confidence that's never been tested."

"Are you saying I'm good for your family's character development?" she teases.

"I'm saying you're good for all of us. Me especially." I kiss her forehead. "Now, should we celebrate this decision properly? I believe there's champagne in my fridge specifically for moments that deserve celebration."

"And after champagne?" The heat in her voice makes my pulse spike.

"After champagne, I plan to show you exactly how much I love every brave decision you make. Starting with this one."

She stands, pulling me to my feet. "Then let's not waste any time. We have a future to build, and I'm finally ready to believe it's real."

As we head inside, I think about how far we've come in three months. From her walking away at the gala convinced she didn't belong, to choosing to move in together despite her fears. From me desperately trying to prove I'd changed, to understanding that loving someone means supporting their healing rather than just benefiting from their healed state.

This isn't the perfect love story where everything is fixed and easy.

But it's real. It's messy. It's two people choosing each other despite their respective damage, building something beautiful out of honest effort and genuine commitment.

And that's better than perfect.

That's worth everything.

Lianne

Six months after the gala breakdown, I stand in my newly organized closet—half my clothes, half Cameron's—getting ready for what I think is just another Saturday dinner at his parents' house.

I've gotten better at these family dinners. Not perfect—I still have moments where I'm hyperaware that I'm the only person at the table who didn't summer in the Hamptons or winter in Aspen. But therapy has helped me recognize when that voice is my trauma talking versus actual reality.

"You almost ready?" Cameron calls from the bedroom. "We need to leave in ten minutes if we want to miss traffic."

"Almost." I'm debating between two dresses when I catch my reflection in the mirror and see the old familiar anxiety creeping into my expression.

Code word time.

"Cameron?" I call out. "Pineapple."

He appears in the doorway immediately. Pineapple—our agreed-upon signal for when my trauma is spiraling, when I need him to talk me down from the ledge my brain is trying to push me over.

"What's the fear?" he asks gently, settling onto the edge of our bed.

"Your dad mentioned bringing business associates tonight. I don't know who they are, what they do, what I'm supposed to talk to them about." I can hear how my voice is getting tighter, faster. "What if I say something stupid? What if they wonder why you're with an event planner instead of someone from your world who actually understands—"

"Stop." Cameron stands, moving behind me so we're both facing the mirror. His hands rest on my shoulders. "Reality check time. What do you actually know?"

This is our pattern now. When I spiral, he walks me through reality versus fear.

"I know I'm successful at what I do," I say, following the script my therapist gave us.

"True. What else?"

"I know you love me and chose me."

"Also true. And these business associates—do they matter more than me?"

"No."

"Do their opinions of you change anything about our relationship?"

"No."

"So worst case scenario—you have an awkward conversation with someone who doesn't understand event planning. Best case scenario?"

"I have an interesting conversation with someone who wants to hire Luminous Events," I admit, feeling my breathing slow.

"There you go." He kisses the top of my head. "You're not that scared foster kid anymore, Lianne. You're a successful businesswoman who happens to be dating someone whose family has fancy dinners. The only person who still sees you as not belonging is you."

"I know. Logically, I know that." I lean back against him. "But sometimes the scared voice is really loud."

"I know. And that's okay. That's what therapy is for, what I'm for—to remind you when your brain is lying." He spins me around to face him. "Now, which dress makes you feel most like yourself?"

I look at the two options. The navy one is more formal, more "appropriate" for his parents' dinner parties. The emerald one is brighter, bolder—the kind of thing I'd wear to my own events.

Six months ago, I would have chosen the navy. Would have picked what I thought they'd expect rather than what I actually wanted.

"The emerald," I say decisively.

"Perfect. You look incredible in green." He pauses. "Though full disclosure, you look incredible in everything. I'm biased."

Twenty minutes later, we pull up to his parents' house in Pacific Palisades. The familiar knot of anxiety tries to form in my stomach, but I breathe through it.

I belong here because Cameron wants me here. That's the only credential that matters.

Mrs. Judd greets us at the door with genuine warmth that still surprises me sometimes. "Lianne, darling, you look beautiful. Is that new?"

"Thank you. Yes, I got it last week."

"The color is perfect on you." She air-kisses my cheek, then whispers, "I'm so glad you're here. These business dinners can be dreadfully boring without someone interesting to talk to."

Six months ago, I would have heard that as condescension—like she was suggesting I was entertainment rather than equal. Now I hear it for what it is: genuine appreciation that I bring different perspective to her usual social circle.

Growth. Actual, measurable growth.

The dinner is exactly what I expected—Mr. Judd's business associates discussing market trends and investment strategies, their wives making polite conversation about charity galas and country club politics. The kind of environment that used to make me feel like an anthropologist studying a foreign culture.

But tonight, I hold my own. When they ask about my business, I talk about the Sterling gala and the Highland fundraiser with confidence rather than apology. When the conversation turns to wine, I contribute knowledge from those Santa Barbara tastings. When someone mentions their daughter is getting married, I smoothly hand them my card without feeling like I'm begging for business.

I catch Cameron watching me with pride, and something warm settles in my chest.

After dinner, his mother suggests we all move to the terrace for dessert and coffee. But Cameron catches my hand.

"Actually, Mom, could Lianne and I borrow the library for a few minutes? There's something I want to show her."

"Of course, darling. Take your time."

The library is my favorite room in this house—floor-to-ceiling bookshelves, comfortable leather chairs, a fireplace that probably cost more than my first car. Cameron's grandfather built this room, and it still smells like old books and expensive scotch.

"What did you want to show me?" I ask as he closes the door behind us.

"This." He pulls a small velvet box from his jacket pocket.

My heart stops completely.

"Cameron—"

"Before you panic, let me say what I need to say." He takes my hand, and I notice his is shaking slightly. "Six months ago, you walked away from me because you didn't believe you deserved to be loved. Because your trauma convinced you that you'd always be temporary, that eventually I'd see what my mother saw and realize someone from my world would be easier."

Tears are already forming because I know exactly what's coming and I'm terrified and thrilled in equal measure.

"These past six months, I've watched you do the hardest work I've ever seen anyone do. Not just building a business or coordinating events—that's impressive but it's not the same." His voice cracks slightly. "I've watched you face your trauma head-on. Go to therapy every week even when it's painful. Learn to recognize when your fears are lying to you. Practice being vulnerable instead of running away."

"Cameron—"

"I've watched you choose bravery over safety every single day. Choose to stay when your instinct is to run. Choose to believe you deserve good things even when your trauma screams that you don't." He opens the box to reveal a stunning solitaire that catches firelight. "And I want to spend the rest of my life watching you continue to grow, continue to heal, continue to become more yourself."

"You're really doing this," I whisper, tears spilling over.

"I'm really doing this." He takes the ring from the box. "Lianne Peralta, will you marry me? Not because you're healed—I know that's ongoing work we'll navigate together. Not because you're perfect—because you're beautifully, messily human. But because you're brave enough to keep choosing love even when it terrifies you. Because you make me want to be someone worthy of that bravery."

I should say yes immediately. Should throw my arms around him and celebrate this moment.

Instead, I hear myself say: "I'm still going to have bad days."

"I know."

"I'm still going to spiral sometimes. Need pineapple moments. Wonder if I really belong at family dinners."

"I know that too."

"And therapy is helping, but my therapist says trauma work can take years. That I might always have triggers, always have moments where I feel like that scared foster kid—"

"Lianne." Cameron's voice is gentle but firm. "I'm not asking you to be healed. I'm asking you to marry me. All of you—the successful businesswoman and the scared foster kid and everyone in between. The version who conquers her fears and the version who sometimes needs to be talked down from ledges. I want all of it."

"Even on days when I'm a mess?"

"Especially on days when you're a mess. Because those are the days when you let me in, when you trust me enough to be vulnerable, when we're actually partners instead of you performing strength you don't feel." He's still holding the ring, still on one knee, patient as ever. "So yes or no? Will you take a chance on building a life with someone who sees all of you and loves all of you?"

The scared voice tries one more time: *What if he's wrong? What if you really don't deserve this? What if—*

But I've learned to recognize that voice now. Learned that it's trying to protect me the only way it knows how—by keeping me from risking rejection.

Except I've also learned that safety without love is just another kind of prison.

"Yes," I say, my voice stronger than I expected. "Yes, I'll marry you. Even though I'm terrified. Even though part of me still can't believe this is real. Even though—"

He slides the ring onto my finger and pulls me down into his lap, kissing me thoroughly enough to silence every fear, every doubt, every trauma-driven protest.

"We're doing this," he says against my lips. "We're actually doing this."

"We're actually doing this," I repeat, looking at the ring on my finger—tangible proof that someone chose me permanently, not temporarily. That I'm not just performing belonging but actually building it.

"Should we tell everyone?" Cameron asks.

"In a minute." I frame his face with my hands, needing him to understand something. "Thank you."

"For what?"

"For being patient while I figured out how to believe I deserve this. For not giving up when I walked away. For understanding that my trauma doesn't make me broken, just human." Tears spill over again. "For loving me enough to wait for me to love myself."

"Always," he promises. "Through every pineapple moment, every spiral, every day when you need reminding that you're enough exactly as you are—I'm not going anywhere."

When we finally return to the terrace, hand in hand, my ring catching the outdoor lights, his mother takes one look at us and bursts into tears.

"Finally!" she exclaims, pulling me into a hug that's surprisingly fierce. "I was wondering when my stubborn son would get around to this."

"You knew?" I ask, surprised.

"Darling, he asked for his grandmother's ring three months ago. We've all been waiting." She pulls back to look at me seriously. "I know I haven't always made you feel welcome. I know my words at that first gala hurt you deeply. But Lianne, you've taught this family something important —that belonging isn't about bloodlines or background. It's about character. And yours is extraordinary."

"Thank you," I manage through tears. "That means more than you know."

The rest of the evening passes in a blur of congratulations and champagne toasts. Mr. Judd pulls Cameron aside for what looks like an emotional conversation. The business associates and their wives offer genuine well-wishes that don't feel performative.

But the moment that breaks me is when Mrs. Judd approaches with her phone.

"I wanted to show you something," she says, pulling up a photo. "I've been volunteering with the Highland Community Center since your fundraiser. Working with some of the older girls who are about to age out, helping them with job interview skills and professional networking."

The photo shows her with three teenage girls, all of them smiling.

"You inspired me," she admits quietly. "Made me realize I'd been wasting my privilege on maintaining social status instead of creating real impact. These girls—they remind me of you. Smart, determined, just needing someone to believe in them." She pauses. "I hope you'll help me do better. Teach me how to support them the way I should have supported you."

"I'd like that," I say, meaning it. "I'd really like that."

Later, in Cameron's car heading back to our place, I can't stop staring at the ring.

"Second thoughts?" he teases.

"The opposite. I'm trying to memorize this feeling— being happy without waiting for something to go wrong. Being excited about the future instead of terrified of it." I look at him. "My therapist calls it 'sitting with joy.' Says it's one of the hardest things for people with my trauma background."

"How's it feel?"

"Scary. But good scary. The kind of scary that means I'm growing, not just protecting myself."

He brings my hand to his lips, kissing my knuckles just above the ring. "I'm proud of you. For all the work you're doing, for all the bravery it takes to stay when your instinct is to run. For choosing this—choosing us—even though it terrifies you."

"I'm proud of me too," I admit. "Six months ago, I

couldn't have said that. Couldn't have acknowledged my own growth without minimizing it or deflecting." I lean my head against his shoulder. "But I'm learning. Slowly, messily, with lots of pineapple moments—but I'm learning."

"That's all that matters. Progress, not perfection."

When we get home, I change into my favorite pajamas while Cameron opens a bottle of champagne. We settle on the couch facing the Pacific, exactly where we had our first real conversation after I showed up at his door six months ago.

"Should we talk about wedding planning?" he asks. "I know you'll want to plan something spectacular."

"Eventually. But not tonight." I curl into his side. "Tonight I just want to sit with this. With being engaged to someone who loves all of me, even the messy parts. With the reality that I don't have to be healed to be worthy of love."

"You never had to be healed to be worthy," Cameron corrects gently. "You were always worthy. You just needed time to believe it."

"I'm still working on believing it," I admit. "Some days are easier than others."

"That's okay. We have our whole lives for you to keep working on it." He kisses the top of my head. "And I'll be here for every single moment—the confident days and the scared days and everything in between."

We sit in comfortable silence, watching moonlight on the Pacific, both of us processing what just happened.

"Lianne?" Cameron says eventually.

"Yeah?"

"Thank you for being brave enough to stay. For not

letting your trauma win. For choosing to build a life with me even when it scares you."

"Thank you for understanding that loving me means supporting my healing, not just benefiting from my healed state." I look up at him. "Not everyone would have the patience for the work I'm doing."

"Then not everyone deserves you." He tilts my chin up to kiss me properly. "But I'm going to spend the rest of our lives earning the trust you're placing in me. Proving that you were right to be brave. Showing you that some good things actually do last."

Later, lying in bed wrapped around each other, I think about how far I've come.

Six months ago, I walked away convinced I'd never belong in his world. Convinced that my trauma made me unworthy of love, that eventually Cameron would see what his mother saw and choose someone easier.

Now I'm engaged to him. Planning a future together. Learning—slowly, with lots of therapy and pineapple moments—that I was wrong about not deserving good things.

I'm still scared sometimes. Still have moments where the foster kid voice tells me this can't last, that I'm temporary, that eventually I'll be sent away.

But I'm learning to recognize that voice as trauma, not truth.

And I'm choosing to be brave anyway.

That's what healing looks like—not the absence of fear, but the decision to love despite it. Not waiting until you're perfect, but accepting that you're worthy of good things even while you're still growing.

"I love you," I whisper into the darkness.

"I love you too," Cameron whispers back. "My brave, beautiful, perfectly imperfect fiancée."

Fiancée. The word still feels surreal.

But for the first time in my life, I'm letting myself believe it's real.

And that might be the bravest thing I've ever done.

I hope you enjoyed Lianne and Cameron's romance! Be a guest at their wedding reception in the bonus story available to read for free at www.subscribepage.com/worththewait

Keep an eye out for Worth the Fight, Elliot's story scheduled for release in the fall 2025!

Stay informed of what I'm working on next and their release dates by visiting my website at lizdurano.com or you can find me on Facebook at @lizduranobooks

SHE HAD THE PLAN.

HE HAD FOREVER.

Cassie's life is mapped out: six months as COO, then back to San Francisco for solo motherhood. No dependencies. No trust.

Until her CEO turns out to be Elliot Walker—her former student who never got over her.

Working together means chemistry they can't ignore. But a hostile board is watching, and her fertility appointment is weeks away.

When everything explodes, someone has to sacrifice. Someone has to be brave enough to fight.

Will she choose the safe plan—or the man who's been waiting eight years?

Second chance CEO romance. Age gap. Forbidden love.

SOME PARTNERSHIPS ARE WORTH THE RISK.

OTHERS ARE DESIGNED TO BREAK YOUR HEART.

Highland Community Center isn't just a building—it's my father's legacy, my neighborhood's heart, and the only home my Filipino-American community has ever known. So when Pierce Enterprises announces plans to demolish Highland for luxury condos, I'm ready to fight.

What I'm not ready for is Declan Pierce himself.

The devastatingly handsome CEO should be easy to hate. Instead, I find myself glimpsing something unexpected beneath his corporate armor—vulnerability that calls to me despite every logical reason to keep my guard up.

When he proposes an unlikely collaboration to find preservation alternatives, I face an impossible choice: trust the enemy who could destroy everything I've fought to protect, or miss our only chance for survival.

OTHER BOOKS BY LIZ DURANO

<u>DIFFERENT KIND OF LOVE: TAOS</u>

Everything She Ever Wanted

Breaking the Rules

Where She Belongs

Other Side of Love (Prequel)

<u>DIFFERENT KIND OF LOVE: NEW YORK</u>

Falling for Jordan

Friends with Benefits

Lucky Charm

<u>LOVE BEACH EVER AFTER</u>

Summer with a Navy SEAL

Merry with a Tycoon

Spring Break with a Bodyguard

<u>CELEBRITY</u>

Loving Ashe

Loving Riley

<u>HOLIDAY ENGAGEMENT</u>

The Replacement Fiancé

The Reluctant Fiancee

ABOUT THE AUTHOR

Although Liz studied Journalism in college, she discovered that she preferred writing fiction over ad copy, and so these days, she writes women's fiction and romance.

She lives in Southern California with her family and Truffles, a senior Chihuahua mix who keeps guard of her writing space and a growing pile of books (and wool for when she needs to spin for inspiration).

You can follow Liz's book adventures by visiting lizdurano.com

facebook.com/lizduranobooks

instagram.com/lizdurano

bookbub.com/authors/liz-durano